DAVID YEARSLEY has been wr
– the first four spent on adult fi
his school days. Now, having
a change of genre. This is Davi   .... s
fantasy book. Exciting, mysterious, magical and funny,
The Mystery of Cloverdaisy Cottage is a wonderful dual-
story adventure.

David's first book, *Winding the Clock Back*, was self-
published in June 2014 to high acclaim. It was a factual
take on the iconic decade of the '60s, and was a tremendous
success not only locally but across the UK. David was also
honoured to be chosen as one of the guest speakers at the
2015 Northwich LitFest.

David is an ex-lawyer (of the gentler kind) and a member
of the Vale Royal Writers Group, Northwich and Daresbury
Authors. He currently lives with his family in Cheshire.

You can connect with David via Twitter @DavidKYearsley.

Best wishes
Jacob

the mystery of cloverdaisy cottage

DAVID YEARSLEY

SilverWood

Published in 2017 by SilverWood Books

SilverWood Books Ltd
14 Small Street, Bristol, BS1 1DE, United Kingdom
www.silverwoodbooks.co.uk

ISBN 978-1-78132-720-3

British Library Cataloguing in Publication Data
A CIP catalogue record for this book is available from
the British Library

Page design and typesetting by SilverWood Books
Printed by Imprint Digital on responsibly sourced paper

In sweet and fun-loving memory of the dearest Mum,
Nan and Great Nanna we shall ever know, who waved
us goodbye one last time on 5 May 2017

Childhood is the most beautiful of all life's seasons.

Author unknown

The Mystery of Cloverdaisy Cottage

Part One – The Haunted Loft

One

End of School Term

It was three o'clock on a bright sunny afternoon in the pretty picture-postcard village of Cloverdaisy. The primary school bell rang time on the end of term, and the summer holidays began. Excited school children ran out of their classrooms, looking forward to the long break.

Two were especially thrilled: best friends, Kate and Clara – clever, pretty girls, full of adventure, fun and compassion. Kate cared about people and always looked for the good in everything – a proper little Pollyanna at times. Clara was similar but generally more reserved, though bright as a button as her name indicated. Both were kind, friendly souls who loved music, especially classical, almost as much as they loved to explore.

At ten years old, Kate was like a big sister to nine-year-old Clara. The two were inseparable both in school, where they sat together, and out of it. Although intelligent, they were not averse to playing a prank or two – 'acting the goat' as Nanna Grace called it. Alike in looks, they were regularly mistaken for twins, and often played tricks on people by pretending to be one another.

The day after the end of term, they would be off to see Kate's nanna, who lived in a quaint thatched cottage alongside Cloverdaisy Farm. The cottage was very old with a lot of character and mystical charm, and was rumoured to be haunted. It would be a real treat, especially as 'Nanna Grace', as she was affectionately known, was going to show them how to bake a Victoria sponge. To add to the excitement, Kate's mum, Ruth, had quietly tipped them off about the creepy old loft that had not been disturbed for decades. No one knew what was hidden up there.

The girls were so thrilled that they could hardly stop talking or thinking about their forthcoming adventure, nor could they sleep properly the night before. They were having a sleepover at Kate's house and, supposedly, an early night. However, as if it were not difficult enough to get to sleep, Kate's two-year-old brother Oliver wandered into the girls' bedroom, looking frightfully funny with his pyjamas on back to front and his hair sticking up like hedgehog spikes.

"'Ate, 'Ate, Cwara," he mumbled, demanding attention. "Can't sweep, can't sweep, wead me storwee."

Kate smiled, but Clara looked puzzled, wondering what on earth he was trying to say.

"Don't worry, Clara, he's learning how to talk, but can't quite sound his 'k's, 'l's or 'r's properly yet."

"Oh, I get it now," Clara replied, tickled pink.

Kate lifted Oliver up, kissed both cheeks and gave him a cuddle, before tucking him into their bed and reading him a fairy tale. It did the trick, and Ollie quickly fell asleep.

Snug as a bug in a rug, he was still fast asleep when Kate's mum Ruth appeared at midnight. She carried him carefully out of the girls' room into his own and laid him gently into his frog-shaped cot, where he slept till morning.

Dawn broke, and with it came the ear-splitting sound of the farmyard cockerel, waking Clara up much too early. She had never got used to being woken by such a piercing noise at quite an unearthly hour. Kate wasn't bothered. To her it was like an alarm clock going off!

The fragrant smell of breakfast stirred both girls to their feet, making them dive swiftly out of bed. Showering and dressing quickly, they raced downstairs, the aroma as mouth-watering as the anticipation of the coming day.

"Morning, daughter. Morning, Clara," greeted Ruth cheerfully. "How are we both this bright, beautiful day?"

"Hello, Mum," replied Kate.

"Morning, Ruth," mumbled Clara, still sounding half asleep. "The barn owls woke us up in the middle of the night, screeching and 'twit, too-wit, too-wooing', and the foxes were barking like wild dogs!"

Ruth laughed. "Tell you're not a farm girl, Clara! Did you not listen more closely to the owls?"

"No, I was too busy trying to get back to sleep."

"Well, if you had done, you might have heard them differently. They were saying, 'Twit-twit-twooooo, breakfast for two!'"

Kate, already munching cereal, knew this little ditty off by heart. Clara, still waking up, didn't quite get it until…the penny dropped.

"Oh, that's witty, Ruth, and I can see you have 'cooked for twooooo."

Giggling, she looked across to where a pile of warm,

honey-soaked pancakes was idling, waiting to be scoffed. There was also porridge, homemade toast and fresh poached eggs, all produce from the farm. Scrumptious! At the end of the breakfast table, Ollie was perched in the high chair, amusing himself with his own porridge. Ruth was trying to persuade him to eat the stuff, not throw it at the wall.

"Wow!" said Clara, rubbing her tummy. "Thank you, Mrs Ruth. Looks like you've been busy."

Ruth laughed and nodded. She felt like royalty being called 'Mrs Ruth'.

"Pleasure, dear, you must both eat properly before you go to Nanna's and explore. Don't forget to ask her first...she might take some persuading."

"We won't," Kate and Clara replied in a duet, before tucking in to the delicious breakfast.

"Nanna's going to show us how to make a Queen Victoria sponge."

"Oh, is she now?" said Ruth with a wry smile. "So you even know who it's named after, do you?"

Silence...until Ruth briefly explained, telling them about the great Queen from the nineteenth century.

After breakfast, the girls swiftly packed what was needed for their day's excursion, including a snack for Samson and Sebastian, the two giant Suffolk Punch horses. Knowing how dark and dusty Nanna Grace's loft would be, Ruth made sure they each took a torch, old tee-shirts, jeans and caps.

Following a hug and a kiss from both Ruth and baby Ollie, and a reminder from Ruth about how to behave politely in front of Nanna, the girls skipped off to the cottage.

Chattering and whistling like two budgerigars, they felt like the whole world belonged to them.

After half a mile they arrived alongside the farm. Thundering across the paddock to greet them, hoping for apples and carrots for their trouble, came Samson and Sebastian. Tremendously powerful beasts, they were as majestic as they were kind and good-natured. Towering above the girls, they bent their heads down like the giant brontosauruses in the film *Jurassic Park*, knowing full well there were treats hidden behind Kate and Clara's backs. In a flash, both horses had spun the girls round by their shoulders like spinning tops and snatched the fruit and veg straight out of their hands. When they realised there were no more treats, they licked the girls' faces instead as if to thank them.

There was all sorts of hustle and bustle going on in the farmyard. A truckload of grunting, frothy-mouthed pigs was off to market, and Shep, the black and white collie dog, had just penned a small flock of sheep for their annual haircuts. Dozens of chickens speckled the paddock, clucking and scraping the ground like feathered metal detectors. Their treasure – big, fat, juicy earthworms. The entire working farm was a hive of activity, including the honeybees buzzing away as they went. A glorious, colourful scene of country bliss.

A large dairy herd of Friesian cows was munching fresh pasture grass, chewing the cud before swallowing it. House martins and swifts pounded the blue sky, zooming and diving like model Spitfire aircraft, catching 'enemy' insects on the wing. It reminded the girls of many delightful books they had read, especially Enid Blyton's. Taking deep breaths, the girls needed no reminding just how fortunate they were to spend their childhood in such charming surroundings. They were truly blessed, as the local vicar would say.

"Nanna would say it was like a country scene from a classic Turner," mused Kate.

"Turner? Turner who?" quizzed Clara. "Only Turner I know is Arthur, the wood turner down the workshop!"

The girls were still laughing hysterically at Clara's words when suddenly the peace and tranquillity were shattered. Boris, the farmyard bull, had bolted from the back of the milking parlour, snorting and roaring like a dragon. He was chasing one of the farm labourers, Len, who was desperately trying to hold him off with a pitchfork. It looked like something from a Wild West show. Failure to stop Boris would spell disaster at worst, a very sore bottom at best.

Something had clearly upset Boris, who was normally quite placid, but Nanna Grace had always told the girls, "Never turn your back on a bull." To prevent himself being gored, Len needed something quickly...water! He managed to grab a nearby hosepipe and turn it full on to the charging animal. The jet was so powerful it was like a water cannon hitting an angry mob – not only did it stop Boris in his tracks, it almost took him off his feet. Not bad for an animal weighing almost a ton! It instantly did the trick, making him U-turn back to his box where he was quickly locked up.

What a close shave! It could have been rather nasty, but what wonderful entertainment. Peace restored, Jack, the farmer, appeared, sliding down from the top of a haystack where he'd scrambled for safety.

"Coward!" the girls shouted, even though they had watched

it all from the top of the mound created by the last outbreak of the foot and mouth disease.

"You two have some room to talk, cowering and laughing up there! Besides, he was chasing me first."

"What happened?" asked Kate.

"One of the young heifers lashed out with her hooves and kicked him right on the backside."

"Oh dear," remarked Clara sarcastically. "I've heard of a bear with a sore head, but never a bull with a sore bum!"

This amused Kate, who added, "He will have to be more choosy then, next time, eh? Or else!"

Kate's comment tickled both girls hugely, even making Jack laugh.

"How are you girls doing, then?" he asked when they finally stopped laughing.

"Very well, ta. How's the aquarium coming on, Jack?"

Jack's expression immediately became wary. His eyes darting from left to right, he changed the subject abruptly.

"You over to Nanna Grace's house? Give her my love, won't you?"

"Will do."

Strolling across to the cottage, Kate and Clara briefly wondered why Jack never wanted to talk about his aquarium. They longed to see it and the magnificent creatures rumoured to live there, but Jack guarded it fiercely. Even Len and the other farm labourers, who knew every inch of the farm, had no idea where it was.

Soon, though, the pleasure of the day took over from the girls' musings, and they twirled through Nanna Grace's wooden gate, wiping their shoes on the damp shaded grass as they went. Both pairs were covered in cow muck. The garden path was long and twisty like a snake, encouraging them to stop frequently and smell the scented flowers, especially the sweet peas and the honeysuckle bush. Magic, pure magic! Better than any French perfume.

Arriving at the quaint, ancient cottage, they 'rat-a-tat-tatted' on the thick oak door, the cast iron knocker ringing out for all it was worth. Then they knocked again, even harder.

Where on earth could Nanna Grace be?

Two

Greetings and Catch-ups

Finally Nanna Grace appeared, resplendent in her Dairy Maid outfit as if she had just finished milking or making butter. She might have been old in years, but she was still young at heart with her glowing, rosy, wrinkle-free face, full head of hair and chestnut eyes shining with her ever-present sense of humour. Fit and active for her age, Nanna Grace helped out on the farm every day except Sundays.

She was absolutely thrilled to see Kate and Clara.

"Hello, Nanna," the girls shouted. Nanna Grace was hard of hearing, but she was stubborn and independent like a lot of people her age and would not wear a hearing aid.

"Hey-up, girls," she shouted back in her Cheshire accent. "I can hear, you know, I'm not deaf! How are you both?" She winked at them as Kate pulled a chair across for her to sit on. Nanna Grace looked weary after the morning's labours.

"Fine, thank you," replied Kate. "Great to be on holiday."

Clara simply nodded, feeling a little bit overwhelmed in front of her friend's grandmother.

"I hear Boris has been playing up again."

"Looked like it," said Kate.

"Those farm lads must stop teasing him. One of these days they'll be sorry if those horns end up in their backsides." This amused the girls. Nanna was clearly on fine form. She switched the radio on and sat down to listen.

"What's that lovely song?" asked Clara, plucking up the courage to speak.

"Ah that, my dear, was one of my late husband's favourites. Gilbert used to serenade me with it when he was being romantic." The girls blushed. "It's called 'Kiss to Build a Dream On' by the late great Louis 'Satchmo' Armstrong." As she spoke, a solitary tear drifted down each cheek. She missed Gilbert dearly; a kind, gentle man, full of mischief and fun. "He always called me his rose. I would pretend to be his Juliet – as in Romeo and Juliet – and recite the full line: 'what's in a name? That which we call a rose...'"

"'...by any other name would smell as sweet,'" the girls joined in. "We know that bit, Nanna," Kate added. "Did it at school recently. It's lovely."

"Yes, it is. Thank you, girls, that's nice. You obviously do know it."

The girls could see that the memories were making Nanna Grace emotional, so they sat down with her and listened further.

"Who's 'Satchmo'?" asked Clara.

"Oh, he was a very successful black American singer and musician, lesser known as 'Pops'. Gilbert was called that too, occasionally. Right, young ladies, how about a drink?"

She had made a jug of real lemonade and gave each

girl a large glassful, which they gulped with relish.

"That was nice, Nanna, not all sickly and sugary like you get from the shops," said Kate hiccupping, having drunk it too quickly. She held out her glass for a refill.

"Not so fast, young lady, how about some sunshine first? It will soon be time for lunch. Before that, though, I will show you how to bake that Victoria sponge I promised. We'll make enough for all the family so everyone can have a piece – including baby Oliver, of course."

"Thanks," said Clara dubiously, worried her diabetic mother would not be too thrilled with a sugary cake.

Nanna Grace read her mind and said, "Don't worry, Clara, I know your mum is diabetic and takes insulin so we won't put too much sugar in it. She controls it well, as I know from Ruth."

"Thanks," Clara replied, this time with relief.

"By the way, girls, how did school finish up?"

In stereo came the reply, "Not bad, thanks."

"Did you do well?"

"Yes, very, but not quite as well with the essay work as our autistic classmate, Little Kenny."

"Oh, why was that?"

Clara jumped in. "We were asked to write a three-page story on our favourite sport. I did tennis and Kate did hockey, which took about half an hour."

"So what did Kenny write about?"

"Cricket. He finished his essay in fewer than twelve seconds, and came top of the class."

Nanna Grace looked puzzled. "Cricket? Twelve seconds? What did he write, girls?"

They paused, looking slightly embarrassed before replying, "Rain…stopped…play!"

"Miss Butterfield, our class teacher, howled and cried with laughter, so much so that she split her sides and ran off to the staff room," added Kate. As confused now as she and Clara had been that day in school, she continued, "Miss then called the other teachers in to tell them, and they were all as bad as her. All you could hear was fits of stupid laughter. They were like hyenas."

By now, Nanna Grace had lost her composure too. Starting with a suppressed giggle, she then clutched her sides, doubling up with laughter, and ran out to the toilet. She had never heard anything as short, clever or as witty, from one so young! Kate and Clara, on the other hand, still couldn't see the funny side. What was so good about it? As the two brightest girls in their class, they had been too embarrassed to ask their teachers or mums.

After several long minutes, Nanna Grace came back, still juddering, dabbing her tears and barely able to speak properly. She eventually said, "Clearly, girls, you don't get the joke, do you?"

"No, Nan, we don't."

"Ah, never mind. One day you will. It's what we grownups call 'dry humour'. It's brilliant, a masterpiece, and he deserves to be top. Good on Little Kenny."

"But he only wrote three words," shouted Clara.

"That's the point!" replied Nanna. "Be gone now. I'll explain later."

"Is it like Robert Frost?" chirped Kate brightly. "You know, Clara, we studied his poems at school."

"Ye-es," said Clara, "but what's he got to do with Little Kenny?"

"Well, he summed up everything he'd learned about life in three words, remember?"

"Yes, I remember, clever clogs," said Clara, laughing. "'It goes on.'"

Kate, shaking her head and chunnering about the fact that Clara had stolen her punch line, grabbed her friend's arm and led her outside. She was, however, still excited by what the rest of the day might bring. Nanna Grace had started to laugh again, so they left her to it, thinking she'd gone completely potty.

"First sign of madness, my mum always says, is when someone starts talking or laughing to themselves," said Clara, which made Kate chuckle.

"Mine always says it's good when we can laugh at ourselves."

As they strolled away into the fresh air, they called, "Bye, Nan," thinking she hadn't heard them.

"Cheerio, girls," she shouted back devilishly. "Hope you do better with silent letters."

This stopped them in their tracks.

"Now what? A word quiz?"

Nanna Grace, still tittering, followed them outside.

"Yes it is, sort of, and stop that wittering! You know what I mean, don't you?"

"Course we do, Nanna, but not now," said Kate. "We've had enough for today and want to gulp some fresh air."

"Phonetics," shouted Clara. "A silent letter in a word. It has its origins in Old English."

"Correct," said Grace. "Well done, wench!"

Kate was not amused by Clara showing off, again. In fact, she was peeved, and was going to say as much until she noticed that Clara had gone in a trance and was white with shock. She looked like she had just been hypnotised. It seemed to have happened after she spoke the words 'Old English'.

An enchanting voice was speaking softly into Clara's ear. "Come and find me, Clara, I am waiting for you patiently. You know where to look. Follow the frog. Let nothing deter you in the quest…"

At that moment, Clara cried out as if demented. "Aaahhh!"

Kate almost fainted, while Nanna ran over, screaming like she'd seen a ghost. It was quite a scene, as if phantom souls had delivered an omen.

Clara's eyes opened before she looked at the skies, asking, "Who are you? Where are you from? What do you want with me?"

There was a pause, then the mysterious voice came back.

"The loft, the loft, go to the loft. Look for the old chest. Seek and ye shall find. All will be well."

Suddenly, Clara snapped out of the spell.

"Wow! Where was I? What happened?"

Nanna Grace hugged her and stroked her face, thinking at first she may have had a fit. Then she said, almost as if nothing had happened, "Well, I don't know what that was all about, girls, but let's continue. You all right, Clara?"

"Think so. No idea what came over me, Nanna. It felt like I was taken somewhere. There was a…"

Nanna Grace stopped her short of saying "voice" as she remembered something Gilbert had said many years ago about mysterious voices up in the loft. Kate was still speechless, but she had already made her mind up to get to the bottom of this.

Determined to restore some equilibrium, Nanna Grace said, "Where was I? Yes, right. Before you two head over to the meadow, give me some examples of phonetics."

Not wishing to be outdone by Clara, Kate piped up with, "Knick, knack, knickers," which started Nanna laughing again.

Then Clara said, "Got my thumb in a plum crumb," which made them laugh even more.

"Right, you two *not* so clever clogs," said Kate somewhat smugly, "let's see how bright you *really* are! Bet I can stump you with this little 'silent' teaser..."

"Try us," said Clara, rather indignantly.

"What part of the body has a silent 'c' and you can eat them?"

Nanna Grace and Clara's mouths dropped open like giant carp.

"Ha-ha, got you," gloated Kate. Completely stunned and perplexed, they both repeated the line, hoping that would provide the answer. Nothing.

"See, you're stuck," said Kate, feeling quite chuffed. "Give up?"

Silence.

"No guesses either?"

More silence.

"Right then, I shall now put you out of your miseries. Muscles, of course!"

"Oh no, what a crafty trick," Clara sighed.

Nanna Grace simply burst out laughing to declare,

"That's a gem granddaughter. Well done. It's clever, Clara, not crafty! Don't be too miffed – *we* lost!"

Several minutes passed before Kate and Clara spoke to one another again before eventually making up. Finally, the girls shouted, "Goodbye," for a second time and wandered down through the garden, out into the gloriously wild hay meadow.

The grass carpeting the fields was soft, lush and warm. There was an abundance of wild flowers, scattered like coloured hundreds and thousands, including rare specimens – bethany, scabious, hypericum and wild orchids. The fragrance was absolutely divine.

Kate and Clara sat down and stared at the tiny loft window, completely transfixed. It reminded them of windows they'd seen in old windmills and castles. Clara even thought she could see a face looking at them. She instantly recalled the voice, which had spoken to her, but said nothing to Kate. Whispering gently to one another, the girls tried to imagine what might be hiding up there. Even though it was near, the loft felt enchantingly far away.

Nanna Grace stepped out yet again, which startled them. "Aren't you off to look at the rest of the animals and wildlife? Isn't that why you came here? As well as to see me, of course."

Bashfully, Kate admitted, "Well, we did, Nan, but we were actually talking about your old loft. We know you never let anyone go up there anymore. Mum says no one has been in it for donkeys' years, but there could be treasure hidden there. We'd love to have a good search and maybe clear it out, perhaps take some things to be valued. They may be worth something. Mum also says that the cottage needs doing up and Pops's headstone could do with replacing…"

"Mum says this, Mum says that, does she? Mum's been saying an awful lot by the sounds of it, Kate. I'll have to have a word with that daughter of mine."

The thought of Ruth being told off, not them for a change, made the girls laugh.

"Not trying to solve your fantasy crimes again, are you, girls? Ruth tells me that you've both been reading detective stories recently." Nanna Grace smiled, then began to reflect. "It's actually forty years or more since the loft had a visit from anyone other than Grandpa Pops…except once. Whenever I asked him why he wouldn't let anyone else up there, he would simply say he wanted to keep the secret to himself. I know you are both clever and inquisitive, but do you really think there is treasure trove hidden there? Curiosity killed the cat, you know."

"Except the one with nine lives," chuckled Kate.

The girls struck an angelic pose. After a long pause, Nanna Grace could no longer resist their innocent charms. She finally broke the silence with a pensive smile, saying, "OK, all right then, but only if you promise to be extra careful where you step. The floorboards will be quite rotten after all this time, and bird droppings and all sorts of rubbish will be everywhere. Go on, go and have a look…after we've made the cake!"

They shot back into the cottage as if Boris the Bull were chasing them now. Cock-a-hoop, they couldn't thank Nanna Grace enough. However, Clara was intrigued by Nanna Grace's comment.

"No one but Grandpa Pops has visited the loft for over

forty years…except once. He wanted to keep the secret to himself. Interesting!"

Although Kate said nothing, the comment had not been lost on her, either.

The afternoon got off to a good start. They enjoyed mixing flour, eggs, butter, baking powder and sugar – not too much – for the cake, before pouring the batter into separate cake tins and placing them in the hot oven, an old log-fuelled Aga. After only a few minutes, the heavenly aroma of baking made their mouths water. Even the burning logs had a lovely woodland fragrance.

The best bit then followed – mixing butter with icing sugar to make the buttercream filling. The other half of the filling would be Nanna Grace's homemade strawberry jam. Hoping she wouldn't see, the girls craftily scooped blobs of the buttercream on the end of a spoon, slurping it off like kittens. Too late – spotted!

"Hey, you two, stop that! There'll be none left for the cake, and you've made the filling too soon."

"Sorry, Nan, we couldn't resist. Delicious!"

"Now then, the cake will be ready in about half an hour, so don't be late back."

The girls gave Nanna Grace big hugs and kisses before changing into their old clothes and putting the caps on. Grabbing both torches, they dashed off like scalded cats, running up three flights of stairs. The loft hatch was high up, so Kate took a broom handle and propped it underneath, pushing the lid across until a crack of light trickled through. Dragging an old stepladder over, she climbed to the top rung and heaved the heavy lid to one side and clambered through. Flopping into a heap on the other side she was quickly followed by Clara.

They switched the torches on and tried to stand up on the creaky, sagging floorboards...good gosh! It was like being on the top of a sinking coal mountain, dark and dingy. Filthy with layers of black dust and old ghost-train cobwebs everywhere, the loft smelled like a chimney sweep's bedroom.

Regaining their balance, the girls rose slowly to their feet, steadying themselves by holding on to one another. A shaft of light filtered through the ancient velvet curtain that hung across the fractured loft window – the same window Kate and Clara had been gawping at from the meadow. It settled on their faces as if they'd been singled out for something special. The shaft of light was the only connection between the outside and the spooky, mysterious world of the loft... a world that Kate and Clara might not come back from!

Three

Ghostly Frogs and Secret Books

"I bet it's haunted up here," said Clara, tripping over a doll and a teddy bear, abandoned decades ago, that looked like they had seen better days. Clara's imagination was running riot. "Look at these, Kate. They might have belonged to the children of royalty. Let's take them down when we go…"

"Dolls and teddy bears? Come off it! Leave them there," Kate replied. "Just watch where you're treading. Remember Nanna told us to be careful. We don't want to crash down and land on her lap, do we?" This made them giggle, but not for long. "Now, let's search for something valuable so she can get rich and pay for everything. Then we'll get out of here – it's giving me the creeps already."

"Me too," replied Clara. "Don't suppose rubbishy old toys are much use anyway."

However, Kate suddenly had other ideas. On closer

inspection, the toys seemed in reasonable condition for their age, and she had heard about old dollies and teddy bears being valued on some TV antiques programme. Might they be worth something? Unseen by Clara in the dimly lit loft, she decided to hide them behind an old writing desk for now.

In the meantime, Clara was crawling like a commando across the fragile floor. Something had piqued her interest – a faint glow coming from a far corner of the loft. What was that in front of her? A frog?

Rubbing her eyes, Clara squinted into the gloom. As her eyes adjusted to the poor light, she realised she had not been mistaken. She was indeed looking at a tiny green and gold frog, glowing faintly and beckoning her closer. Must be seeing things, she thought.

Glancing over her shoulder to see if Kate had noticed him, Clara could barely make out her friend. From what little she could see, Kate seemed busy, fiddling with the toys on the other side of the loft. Turning back to the frog, who was now very real, Clara found him jumping up and down with impatience, gesturing frantically that she should hurry up. Intrigued, Clara continued commando style until she was face to face with him. His golden glow increased as he puffed out his chest and proudly motioned towards a heap of old moth-eaten clothes piled on top of something, then Wuff! He vanished into thin air.

Clara gulped in surprise. Wide-eyed, she took deep breaths to steady her nerves, but began coughing as the dusty air in the loft choked her lungs. She then pulled the old clothes aside to find an ancient chest.

"Incredible, the old chest," Clara whispered, a bit too loudly.

"This must be the one the mysterious voice spoke about."

"What was that?" called Kate.

"Nothing," Clara replied hastily, shining her torch on the chest and staring in disbelief.

On one side were ancient words in a style that she knew from an old history book – Old English again. Quivering with fear, Clara lifted the lid up and peered inside. The chest was crammed with classic books from years gone by. Reaching inside, hands trembling, she pulled one out. As she did so, she heard husky, heavy breathing – the mysterious voice again.

"At last, you've found me."

Though nervous on hearing the voice once more, Clara felt less frightened than the first time, so she stared even more closely into the chest. On a small dust cover, she read, "The personal property of Gilbert Gladstone" – Nanna Grace's husband.

She took out the books, one by one. To her absolute joy, she carefully turned over antique copies of *The Wind in the Willows, The Lion, the Witch and the Wardrobe, Pollyanna* and *Alice's Adventures in Wonderland*.

How delightful, she thought, some of my very best favourites, and Kate's.

Then, right at the bottom of the chest, as if deliberately hidden, nestled a bundle of typed chapters called *The Amazing Adventures of Tad Pole and Tommy Frog*, by...

"Kate! Kate, come here, quickly!" Clara hollered. Dropping the last of the old toys in their hiding place behind the desk, Kate crawled over, worried in case something was wrong.

"Keep your voice down," she grumbled. "Nanna might hear us and wonder what on earth's going on. Are you all right?"

"Yes, of course I am...er, well, just about. Look at these gems!" Clara said nothing of the voice. Kate would think her nuts if she did so. "Didn't Nanna Grace once say that Grandpa Pops had written a children's book? Well, this could be it. Look, it has to be! Be quick, the torch batteries are going."

Kate held the manuscript up in the air and shone the dimming torch on the cover, staring at it in muted disbelief.

"Wow, this must be it," said Kate. "Bits of it are coming back. Apparently he became quite poorly after he wrote it and felt shy about contacting an editor he had met at the library. Mum said her name was Fiona. She was extremely excited when Pops told her about the manuscript and offered many times to come round and do an edit, but he always put her off. Nanna Grace said Pops thought there was something fishy about her. She always had an inkling that the manuscripts were discretely hidden by Frank the farmer – Jack's dad and a close friend of Pops. I'm told he was quite a character: a giant of a man with a cherry-red face and enormous plate-like hands. His muck-stained trousers were kept up with a pair of braces long enough to cradle his best sow, and…"

"Hold on a bit, Kate, can't all this wait? Sounds like you're writing a play!"

"Sorry, getting a bit carried away then. But that was probably the last time the loft had a visit."

"Yes," replied Clara. "Remember what Nanna Grace said?"

"I wonder what Pops's secret was," said Kate. Clara remained quiet, thinking that it might have something to do with mystical golden frogs!

"I bet she would love to see this," Kate continued. "Mum said Grandpa Pops had a thing about pond life, especially frogs and tadpoles. Magical ones that could talk."

Clara's brain was working overtime.

"Magical frogs that can talk? I…"

Stopping abruptly, Clara realised that Kate would think her completely crazy if she said she'd seen a golden frog beckoning her across the loft. Bad enough that she could hear ghostly voices.

"But what about this book?" she said, changing the subject. "Was Pops a magician – the Pied Piper or something?"

"Merlin 2, perhaps?" said Kate, which started them giggling. "I don't know. He was lots of things to lots of people."

Lost in the moment as emotions took over, Kate started to sob, but she tried not to show it, especially in front of her best friend. Grandpa Pops was deeply and lovingly missed by all the family, especially Nanna Grace. Clara rather sweetly passed her a soot-stained handkerchief.

"I do remember another special thing, courtesy of Mum," said Kate, pointing towards the ancient writing desk behind which she'd hidden the toys. "He acquired that desk over there in quite peculiar circumstances from the vaults under the remains of the Old Vale Royal Abbey, on the side near the Nun's Grave. It was thought one of the secret tunnels from the Abbey led to the cellar of Nanna's cottage."

"Cellar? The cottage has a cellar as well?" asked Clara.

"Yes," replied Kate excitedly. "It's rumoured that several tunnels lead from the Abbey to the surrounding area including the farm and cottage – but no one's ever been able to find them. The Abbey is soaked in history– our teacher has a fascinating book about it. There was a nun called Ida.

At the time, rumour had it that she was in a forbidden relationship with the abbot, Peter, who was a Cistercian monk."

"Go on," said Clara, excited and scared.

"The Cistercian monks were on good terms with the nearby Franciscan friars, whose order was founded by Saint Francis of Assisi. Remember we did him in RE?"

"Yes," said Clara. "Get to the good bits, please!"

"Well, 'they', whoever 'they' are, say that Saint Francis could talk to animals, reptiles and birds and felt at one with all creation. Mum says it gave Grandpa a wonderful idea to write a story about pond creatures that could talk with one another, and humans too..."

"Like Doctor Doolittle?"

"Yes, only I think the frogs could perform magic as well. Anyway, this writing desk is said to have contained papers possibly written by the great Saint himself, or even King Edward I who founded the Abbey after a dream. It was that bit which intrigued dear old Pops. When he heard that the Abbey was selling off ancient artefacts, he was determined to get the desk and whatever was in it."

"That's all very interesting," said Clara, "but what's it got to do with Pops's story?"

"A lot, actually," replied Kate. "Mum told me that as soon as the old writing desk came into his possession, he found he could talk to animals. Just like Saint Francis."

"No!" hollered Clara.

"Be quiet!" whispered Kate, worried. "Nanna Grace might think we're in trouble. She will order us down if she hears any more noise. Besides, the cake will be ready now."

Calming down, Kate continued, "Nanna Grace often

said to Mum that Grandpa's story was set in real life and based around a village pond which suffered serious flooding years ago. Amphibians escaped to their new home, a glorious enchanted pond, through a tunnel near an old acorn tree, led by the magical Golden Frog. The Golden Frog also makes predictions about the future, and the pond is said to be haunted…"

"Like this loft," whispered Clara.

"What do you mean?" asked Kate, looking sharply at her friend.

"Oh, nothing," said Clara, shaking the dust off her clothes ready to go back down the stepladder. "Can you smell the cake now?"

"Yes, I can. Yummy! Come on, we'd better go, quickly. Can't expect Nanna Grace to bring it up here, can we?"

Chuckling, Kate carefully placed the manuscript back in the old chest, before they both scrambled down the ladder and rushed back into the kitchen. Excited and out of breath, both girls were ready to break the news.

Four

The Magic Manuscript

Nanna Grace was tapping her watch. The cake was nearly ruined, burnt almost black! Then she stared at Kate and Clara, aghast. They looked like two Victorian chimney sweeps, covered in soot and grunge and almost matching the colour of the cake.

"Come on, you pair, what have you been doing till now? Take those filthy clothes off and wash your 'chopses!'

"Chopses?" they answered in unison. "What are those, Nanna?"

"Your two lovely, sweet faces, girls, when they're clean. It's a colloquialism."

They looked at one another, puzzled.

"It means a word that's only used locally. You won't find 'chopses' in your dictionary."

"Thanks, Nanna Grace," said Clara. "It sounds amusing and friendly."

"It does," said Kate.

Following a wash and change of clothing, the girls scoffed generous portions of the just about edible cake once the filling had been put in. They barely uttered a word, until Kate broke the silence and raised the subject of Grandpa's lost manuscript.

"Nanna, do you remember that children's book Grandpa supposedly wrote decades ago?"

"Yes, love, bits of it, about some Golden Frog and a Magical Tadpole who saved all the pond life from tragedy or something. I'd give anything to see it. If only that old manuscript could be found."

The girls smiled smugly.

"It would mean such a lot and remind me of all the good times. Besides, I would love to know what the whole story was about and how it ended."

"Wait there!" yelled Kate. She wriggled into her dirty clothes again and darted back up the stairs to the loft and across to the old chest. Anxious moments ticked by, until she returned to the kitchen table, clutching the manuscript as if it were the Holy Grail.

Clara patted her on the back. Nanna, sensing she was about to see something special, delved through the kitchen drawers, trying to find her reading glasses. Making her jump, Kate ceremoniously plopped the faded manuscript right in front of her. Taken completely by surprise, Nanna Grace was flabbergasted. Locked-in emotions ran wild as her tears flowed, running fast down her rosy-red and wrinkle-free face like tiny waterfalls. She produced her handkerchief – a clean one!

"My, oh my, look at all these lovely old pages of Pops's book. My dear Pops. Bless you, dear husband, bless you so much. What an absolute joy."

Slowly flicking the pages, she murmured, "How delightful. The words are still legible even after all these years. He stored it well, girls."

Clara nodded. "He certainly did, Nanna Grace. I found it underneath a pile of old books in a rickety old chest." She paused, expecting to hear the mysterious voice again, but nothing came. "Kate was studying, or should I say fiddling with, old dolls and teddy bears abandoned in one of the corners." The comment made Nanna twitch a bit. Kate clocked her reaction, wondering if Nanna Grace knew something about the toys' history or value, but was not letting on. Clara read her mind and continued. "The chest was labelled 'Property of Gilbert Gladstone' and there was another name barely legible on the front cover of the manuscript: Molly Benjamin, or something. That's as far as I got. I didn't want to carry on in case I spoiled something."

"That was most kind, Clara, thank you. Yes, that's all possible, girls. It's so hazy now. I do recall Frank the farmer, Pops's close friend, hauling boxes up there ages ago. He even got lost! Frank was quite a character – once seen, never forgotten. He was Jack's father, and…"

"I know," said Clara. "I can almost picture him. Kate started to describe him in the loft. Said Ruth had told her ages ago."

"He could spin a good yarn, too. But he wasn't kidding when he came down from the loft all those years ago. That was the only time it was disturbed. Ashen-faced, he was. Said he was never going up there again. He'd heard voices and was frightened to death."

Clara froze. So, she wasn't the only one, who'd been haunted in the cottage's eerie loft.

"Pops was shy about the manuscript when I asked him. He would mumble, 'One day, you might get to read the story. It's about a magic frog – a very special one.' I thought he was going crackers, or he and Frank had been drinking again. However, never thought this would happen. I didn't expect to live long enough to see it. The story lines – what little I recall – might be too advanced, even for you two gifted girls. Then again, how do we know without reading it? Would you want to read it?"

"Yes, of course we would, Nanna. It would be a pleasure and a privilege," said Kate, knowing in her heart that Nanna Grace would love to hear the story and spoken properly, just like Pops would have done all those years ago. "I'll read it out loud, if I may. I've heard pieces from Mum's memory. She said the story was based on real life. Grandpa Pops used to tell Mum titbits from it, but she thought it was just a yarn to get her to sleep, so never took it seriously. However, she remembers he was very convincing and she never really got it out of her head."

"That's right, he was," said Nanna Grace. "Well remembered, dear, it's coming back a tad now. There was a Cloverdaisy Pond. All the animals would have perished there in the Great Village Flood, were it not for the guile and genius of Frank's son, Jack."

On hearing the name Jack, the girls stared at one another. Clara whispered, "So Jack must be the one who started the aquarium, and helped rescue the pond creatures too?"

"I wonder why he wouldn't talk to us about it in the farmyard earlier," Kate whispered back.

Nanna Grace continued, "Jack used to breed and conserve rare amphibian pond life. Grandpa always said, though, that he was not the real hero who inspired him to write the manuscript in the first place. He created the story in order to put the record straight. Reckons he could talk to the pond life and they told him what had really happened. 'Weird, spooky,' I used to say, but Pops was always deadly serious. Because of the mystery, he used a pseudonym."

"What's a pseudonym, Nan?"

"A pen name, or nom de plume as it's also called. Pseudonyms are adopted by authors who want to remain anonymous, like the Brontë sisters and George Eliot."

Both girls looked completely baffled.

"Who's George Eliot, Nan?" asked Kate. "We haven't studied him at school yet."

"You haven't studied her," corrected Nanna Grace. "George Eliot was a woman."

The girls shrieked with laughter.

"A woman called George?"

"Yes dear, for book purposes. Her real name was Mary Ann Evans."

"So why...?"

"She used a man's name because she thought her books wouldn't be taken seriously if everyone knew she was a woman. She wrote seven novels: three in particular are quite famous, *Middlemarch*, *The Mill on the Floss* and *Silas Marner*."

"So if George Eliot had to pretend to be a man to be taken

seriously, why did Grandpa Pops pretend to be a woman?"

"Grandpa Pops had read that male writers of children's stories should pretend to be women so they would be more successful," Grace continued. "Look up Evelyn Waugh too. Now there's an author. 'Better chance of being published,' Pops would grumble. I didn't agree, and still don't. Look at all the past greats. I wouldn't be surprised if Pops had stored some classic children's books in the loft too."

The girls couldn't believe their ears, having seen plenty of books by past greats tucked inside the chest.

"All I ever wanted was for him to get some credit under his real name. Mind you, as I get older, I'm beginning to understand it better. I don't know where the Benjamin so and so written on the front comes from…Wait a minute. Pops liked classical music, Benjamin Britten especially. Could be that? Anyway, Molly was his mother's Christian name. Everyone called her 'Our Moll'. I wouldn't be surprised if that 'pops' up somewhere – 'scuse the pun! They were very close. He may have had something else in mind, like a tribute to her. However, I am longing to hear the full story, girls, so let's continue. Soon be milking time again."

Just as they were settling down, there was a loud rat-a-tat on the back door, before it opened on its own. In sauntered Ruth with baby Ollie fast asleep in his buggy.

"Hello, everyone," she boomed cheerfully.

"Hello, Mum."

"Hello, Ruth."

"Hey-up, daughter," said Nanna Grace in her broad Cheshire accent. "What a nice surprise!"

"Having a good day?" Ruth continued. "You two look

cosy – having fun? I was beginning to wonder where you'd got to!"

"Yes, we are," replied Kate. "Loads, and guess what, Mum?"

"Go on. Don't tell me…you burnt the cake?"

"Not quite!"

"Milked the cows? Did all the housework? Made the tea?"

"No, no! Nanna let us go up into the loft."

"Did she now?"

"You wouldn't believe what we found."

"Dead cat? Pigeon's nest? Million pounds? Ghosts?"

Clara went pale when Ruth mentioned ghosts, but Kate didn't notice.

"No, Mum!" she said, exasperated. "Stop teasing us. Tell her, Clara."

Clara pulled herself together and turned to face Ruth with a grin.

"It was much better than that, Ruth."

"Yes, it certainly was," Nanna Grace piped up. "Come and sit down. You're in for a real treat, daughter. The girls actually found your late father's book manuscript. That children's story. It was hidden in an old chest."

"Pardon?" Ruth replied. "You found what? Did I hear right, Mum?"

"Yes, you did, my dear."

"The girls found…I thought you said that…you're kidding! Never!" Ruth burst out crying then fell backwards on to the sofa, shocked but pleasantly surprised.

"They did. Look here."

"Oh my word, how incredible. What a lovely surprise. Absolutely brilliant, girls, well done."

"Isn't it just?" said Grace. "Now, make yourself cosy. Kate's going to read it as a family read…with Clara present, of course. Settle down and listen to our storyteller. Right, granddaughter, over to you. Please continue."

Kate recomposed herself, this time at the top of the table. She sat upright, prim and proper, like a TV newsreader, before clearing her throat. Then she placed Pops's manuscript in front of her. Taking deep breaths, she started by announcing the title and author's pen name, Molly Benjamin, nodding to Nanna Grace in the process, who simply smiled approvingly. Pops had never forgotten his dear old Mum.

Ruth was beaming with emotion and still in tears. With one arm around her and the other round Clara, Nanna Grace leaned back and cuddled them both. Even her two favourite farm cats joined them, purring and adding to the cosiness. She then closed her eyes and pretended to hear her late husband's voice as Kate started to read sedately in her best Radio 4 tone.

"The Amazing Adventures of Tadpole and Tommy Frog…"

the Amazing Adventures of Tadpole and Tommy Frog

by Molly Gilbert

The Amazing Adventures of Tadpole and Tommy Frog

Part One – The Premonition of Danger

One

Stars of the Show

One fine summer's morning in the pretty village of Cloverdaisy, the marsh and lily pond at the bottom of Longmeadow started to ripple and sway in the gentle breeze. Curves of mixed colours appeared in a bright archway: red, orange, yellow, green, blue, indigo and violet, mimicking the rainbow. Sunshine lit the water from the blue sky high above.

All of a sudden, slow jerking movements made the top of the pond shuffle and shake like a large, wobbly jelly. Moments later, tiny fish-like creatures with black heads and small tails broke away from the grey jelly-ball. They had been living in frogspawn: thousands of eggs, laid by the female frog. The jelly-ball had been home for weeks to the small creatures that now had a name: tadpoles! They squeezed out of the frogspawn to start life on their own.

Darting back and forth like water boatmen, the tadpoles moved faster and faster – zip, zoom, zap – until one of them, whose name was Tad, swam away on his own. He wiggled, full of himself, before swishing towards the edge of the pond to catch his breath. He had gone too far, too fast.

"Phew!" he gasped, breathless from all the activity. However, this tiny, tiddly creature was no ordinary tadpole. Even though he looked just like his brothers and sisters from the spawn, he was much bigger, and he had been blessed with magical powers – ones he didn't yet know about. His sibling tadpoles were making plans for their futures, but these sounded boring to Tad. He would have fun, excitement and adventure while he was still young. His mission in life was to enjoy himself and not regret one moment.

After a short while floating and resting, he looked back at what had been his home. He was surprised to see all the jelly-balls had now broken up. The other tadpoles were scurrying everywhere, but had no idea where they were going. Fascinated, yet amused, Tad wondered what would happen next.

Suddenly, right beside him, came a splish, splash, splosh. A small greenish creature with a tiny head and hands, funny feet and the remains of a tail appeared on one of the large lily pond leaves.

It was a young frog.

Oooohhh, thought Tad, he's different!

"What's your name?" he asked.

"Tommy," croaked the frog.

Tad couldn't take his eyes off him.

"Hello, funny looking Tommy Frog. Where did you jump

from? I've just left the frogspawn, but you haven't. You're too big!"

Tommy was so startled by Tad's cute, bubbly voice that he fell back into the pond – splosh!

Tad laughed, making small chuckle bubbles plop from his tiny oval mouth. Tommy quickly surfaced and found himself face to face with the grinning tadpole.

"I come from the pond and used to live in frogspawn, but who are you, making me jump like that?"

"I'm Tad, the new born tadpole, small and sweet. I also live here in the pond. Mr Tommy Frog, would you please be my friend? Pleeeaase?"

"I'd love to be your friend, but," the frog took a bow, "just call me Tommy."

"Thank you, Mr…er…Tommy," said Tad, trying to bow himself but falling over as he did so.

"I will look after you like a big brother," croaked Tommy as he bent down and gave Tad a big squelchy hug.

"Thank you so much," replied Tad. "That felt nice. It's great to have an older brother. All of mine are the same age, but not as handsome as you. Are we related?"

"Ha-ha, we might be," chuckled Tommy. "You have a great sense of humour, just like me. Have you eaten, Tad? I'm feeling quite peckish."

"No, I haven't."

"Let's find some grubs to eat to put us in good fettle."

"An excellent plan, Tommy, then why don't we have one big adventure for ever? We were told when we left the frogspawn about a wonderful rainbow up in the sky and a crock of gold at the end of it. Maybe we can find it together, eh?"

Tommy began to cry tears of joy. He was keen to have an exciting new friend like Tad, so he leaned over and hugged him again.

"Yes, maybe we can. Come over here, Tad Pole, let me show you around. The adventure starts right now! We'll tour the entire pond and marshes. I'll slide into the water and you can saddle ride on my back."

Tad was over the moon, thrilled to bits. What a trip this would be! He slithered on to Tommy's back and held on tight. Off they splashed and sploshed, up and down like the Big Dipper. They laughed and croaked loudly, waving greetings to everyone around the pond.

"This is great fun," puddle-croaked Tad. "But where exactly are we going?"

"To catch juicy grubs, my friend – insects and larvae, newly hatched wingless wormlike things before they change."

"Before they change?" Tad was confused. "Aren't they nice enough as they are?"

"Ha-ha!" Tommy laughed, shaking his head and doing his best to keep Tad on his back. "The change they go through is called meta-morph-o-sis," he said, spelling the long word out so Tad might understand it better. "It's a big word, but my mum told me it means something life changing. We frogs go through the same process…did you know?"

"What?" shouted Tad, almost falling off Tommy's back. "Do you mean one day you'll look like me?"

"No," replied Tommy, laughing so much that Tad did fall off this time. Tommy quickly scooped him up with his front legs and gently placed him back. "You will look like me, not the other way round. Some weeks ago, I was the same as you. When you get to my age, you don't change very much, although even I haven't quite finished growing yet."

"Thank goodness for that," said Tad, unsure and a bit nervous of the process Tommy was describing. "What else do we eat, Tommy?"

"Other grubs, grasses and flying insects, but never one of our own, little fella."

"What a relief," replied Tad, smiling. "We are family, not cannibals."

"Now, when I get super hungry, I treat myself to some tasty bluebottle pie and waffle-worms with wild honey."

"I quite fancy that," croaked Tad, his tiny belly rumbling like a baby volcano.

"You will do," said Tommy. "It's natural. We can't survive or grow without food, or the fresh drinking water we swim in. But be careful. Watch out for Neville the Nasty Newt and Ferocious Fiona the Giant Carp. Both are crafty and have huge mouths. Fiona's is so big she could eat anything!"

"Oh dear," sobbed Tad. "I don't want to be eaten by Nasty Neville or Ferocious Fiona. In fact, I don't want to be eaten at all."

"Don't worry, little brother, you won't, wait and see. In the meantime, I'll protect you."

"Thanks very much for that, Tommy."

"No problem, little friend. We'll all be thanking you in time."

Tad looked at him, confused, but Tommy continued speaking before he had a chance to ask any questions.

"Now, Neville looks like a cross between a water lizard and a young crocodile, and is very sneaky. He has a head like mine, but with a crest on top. His body is much longer with a lizard-like tail, and he sports a golden belly with black spots on it."

Tad tried to memorise everything. Neville sounded like something out of a jungle swamp, not the local pond.

"He also has four claw-like feet, good eyesight and swims extremely fast. Fiona is slower, but her mouth is so huge, it could suck the whole pond up. She looks like a lazy so and so and is shaped like a squashed kipper-fillet with a curved head and a tiddly wedge-shaped tail. Don't be fooled, though. She can spin round faster than a Catherine wheel. Whatever happens, don't do a Jeremy Fisher on us and slide into the pond without looking or she'll have you."

"Who's Jeremy Fisher? What's a Catherine wheel?"

"He's a character in a well-known children's book by a famous lady author called Beatrix Potter. I heard the school kids talk about her as I lozzucked by the edge of the pond. He was also a frog. A very handsome one, too." Tommy puffed his chest out with pride as he said this. "Oh, the Catherine wheel, that's a firework," he continued. "Do you know, I have a strange suspicion that you will end up bigger than me one day. We are different shapes now, but we have much in common. However, until you can look after yourself properly, you must be vigilant, especially when swimming on the surface. You could also be eaten by other pre-da-tors, like the pike and perch fish and birds of prey who dive from the air – herons and hawks, and even Oscar the Owl."

Tad nodded, unsure why he should fear an owl called Oscar. Besides, he didn't know what an owl was. Right now, he loved Tommy's company – so much so that he somersaulted off the top of the water with great excitement and joy.

Before they set off again, both took forty winks on the shady, snoozy side of the water – a pond nap. Several sweet dreams later, Tad Pole and Tommy Frog woke up, yawned, then slithered back into the pool and continued their journey. Tad clung tightly to Tommy's back, gurgling and bubble-blowing as they zoomed along. The speed spray kept them moist and stopped their delicate skins from drying out.

Tommy felt like a circus acrobat on a magical fairground ride as they jumped from leaf to leaf. "Whoopee, whoop woo," he chortled. They hurtled through the air until his little legs ached from all the jumping. Pausing to catch his breath, he spotted some giant gnats heading their way.

"Gnats are succulent for young frogs and tadpoles," Tommy said, smacking his lips as he watched them. Flying alongside were some tasty looking fruit flies too. It would be like dinner and dessert all in one go!

"Look, Tad, could be our first meal together."

Then, slobbering and salivating, Tommy prepared to pounce. Out of the blue, taking poor Tad by surprise, he launched into the air like a killer whale. He landed smack bang in the middle of the food cloud, catching huge mouthfuls of gnats and flies as he did, before landing back in the pond…hard. Tad was clinging on for dear life, until he could hang on no more. He tumbled off and sank down, deep into the pond. Disaster!

Tommy quickly returned to where he had lost Tad, chewing the insects as he went.

"Tad, Tad," he hollered tearfully, not realising that as soon as he opened his mouth, the rest of the food would fly out. Sad though it was to see it disappear, he turned his attention back to Tad who was far more important. "I must find him quickly before Fiona and Neville do."

Upset at his friend's sudden departure, Tommy

dive-bombed into the pond. He swam deeply to find his little lost pal. Although he was an excellent swimmer and rapidly scoured the murky pond bed for signs of life, he found nothing. He came back up, took massive breaths and dived straight back down again.

The pond was deeper than he'd thought it would be, making Tommy a bit anxious. Then he had a brainwave – a brilliant idea that had worked before. Knowing where all the newts and carp fish would be lurking, he generated hundreds of air bubbles with the remaining oxygen left in his lungs then shot back to the surface. He gripped the edge of a lily leaf to recover.

Time was running out. Would Tad appear?

Suddenly, there was a shudder and a ripple of water. Then a quivering little head quietly plip-plopped above the surface. It was Tad...alive! Tommy's air bubbles had carried him from the bottom of the pond to the top. Once there, he had managed to crawl quietly but wearily on to the lily leaf where Tommy was resting.

Tommy hadn't spotted Tad yet. Sad and sighing, he began to cry. Tad, full of mischief, decided to creep up behind him, then shout, "Boo hoo, it's me!" Tommy shot up in the air like a Jack-in-the-box, startled and surprised but glad to see Tad.

"Tad, Tad – thank heavens you're alive. I was so worried, thought you were a goner." Then he gave Tad a big, sloppy hug. Tad simply smiled, grateful for the affection. Tired and worn out from the day's exertions, they both fell fast asleep again.

*

Another hour slipped idly by and it was soon dusk. The two friends woke, even hungrier than they had been before. With Tommy's food flying off and Tad not even getting a crumb, they had to find more to eat, quickly.

They looked across the pond, then stared at the changing sky. The insect clouds had long gone. However, Tommy was blessed with perfect night vision and excellent hearing – attributes which would ensure they would eat, and soon.

"Where's all the food gone?" groaned Tad. "I'm so hungry now, I could eat a seahorse."

This made Tommy laugh. "Just a moment," he said, "I've spotted something."

There in the dimming light hovered small clusters of red lily beetles and midges. They were circling and clinging around the top of a three foot high poker reed

"What tasty morsels," Tommy whispered, smacking his rubbery lips as he did so.

"What's a m-o-r-s-e-l?" asked Tad, spelling out the word so he could say it better.

"A morsel is a tasty piece of food," Tommy croaked softly. "The beetles and midges are too high up for you to see. Wait here quietly and be very still. Don't fall in this time!"

"Promise I won't," said Tad, hopping across to a nearby lily leaf where he could watch Tommy. "Hope you catch them, my tummy's really rumbling now."

The young frog had heard, but was already gone. He swam stealthily to the base of the reed and focused on catching their supper.

Tad said a little prayer. He had no idea what it would do, but it made him feel happy.

Tommy crept super-quietly up the poker-shaped stem

of the reed like a praying mantis. Without warning and as fast as lightning, he pounced.

Bang, zoom, squash, splosh, snap! He bagged the lot then crashed back into the water. He swam to where Tad was waiting, but kept his mouth shut this time. However his plan was almost scuppered when a wasp flew across and stung his head.

"Ouch!" he wanted to yell, but this time he realised if he did so, the banquet would fly off again. He winced instead.

Tad was thrilled to bits when he saw Tommy's mouth stuffed with food. "Yippee, hoorah!" he squealed.

Tommy simply winked, sliding on to one of the giant pond leaves and mashing the food up so they wouldn't get indigestion.

"Well done, Tommy, you were brilliant. So fast, too," chuckled Tad, excitedly.

"Thank you. Tuck in."

They feasted heartily like frog royalty. It was scrumptious! After such a delicious meal, the pair lay back with full bellies and snoozed.

It was pitch black when their eyes opened. Although the day had ended, their adventure hadn't. Nature was full of surprises: sounds and creatures that only came out after dark.

"Umm," said Tad, feeling nervous. "I've never seen the world like this before. Are we all right here, Tommy?"

"This is the same place as it was in daylight, but the darkness brings out another world. If you need more to eat, just let me know. You're growing. We must keep your strength up. It's been a long, busy day, but enjoyable."

Despite needing sleep himself, Tommy was ever wary of danger. As the pond predators hardly slept, he needed to take Tad to a safe place, and quickly. Some days earlier, he had constructed a maze leading to a secret camp made from pond reeds, twigs, small stones and thick, heavy mud – a 'froggy' den just below a giant lily leaf by the side of an abandoned swan's nest. The cool night water lapping into it would keep them moist and comfortable, and reed pipes would act as oxygen tanks bringing air from the surface to save them coming up. More importantly, they'd be protected from predators. It was like a fortress. Nothing except frogs and tadpoles could get in or out without drowning or getting stuck.

Without further ado, Tommy gently lifted Tad on to his back and swam down through the maze into the den. Once there, he laid Tad on a leafy sponge bed, then kept watch.

"I'm weary," said Tad softly.

"Me too," croaked Tommy. "Turn in and get some sleep. Snooze and slumber…"

Before Tommy had finished, Tad had drifted off. Tommy waited before doing the same, but kept one eye half open.

Tad's day, which had started so dramatically, now ended serenely in a safe, comfy bed. As he slept, he dreamed of Utopia – a special, tranquil place; a frog and tadpole paradise called Frogstock Pond where all creatures could live in peace and harmony, including owls, fish and newts. He shuddered – even the enemy? Perhaps it was not such a nice place, after all. Despite the ever-present danger, though, he knew something special would happen soon.

He didn't know how he knew; he just knew.

A song played lucidly in his dreams – two full-grown frogs were singing a beautiful duet in Frogstock Pond. It was somewhere he had never visited before, yet it felt so divine, so heavenly. He could almost be there…

> Long ago and far away,
> I dreamed a dream one day,
> And now that dream is here beside me…

Tad awoke with a start. A dream? Feeling strange, mysterious power surging through him, he was sure he'd just experienced something far more important than a mere dream. It would indeed, one day, 'be here beside him'.

Two

A New Tail

Tad woke early and thought of his chance meeting with Tommy the day before and what was to come. Was it really just a coincidence that they'd met? After his strange dreams the previous night, Tad wasn't sure there was any such thing as coincidence. He wasn't sure why yet, but he knew that there was something different about him. Something he had to do.

Puffing out his chest as much as a tadpole could, Tad made a silent promise: when the moment came for him to shine, he would make sure he was ready. Happy and cheerful with his resolution, he sat by the edge of the pond and sang an English country song:

Early one morning
Just as the sun was rising,

I heard a young maiden
In the valley below.

Daybreak greeted the wildlife with a dense mist, covering the whole of Cloverdaisy Pond. It was like a blanket, soft and comforting. The sun rose slowly from its slumber, glowing like a giant red and white balloon. Beams of sharp sunlight sliced the mist into fluffy little cotton wool balls, and with them came the dawn chorus. Birdsong broke out everywhere; a mass of whistling and warbling chorused through the trees, hedgerows and meadow grass. The sun smiled and shone even more brightly. Beauty kissed and hugged the earth like a long-lost friend.

Tommy, wide awake now too, started his early morning exercises, and Tad joined in. Stretching and bending their silky, slippery bodies in time with the chuff-chuff of a steam train passing close by, they felt glad to be alive.

Their tummies rumbled. "What's for breakfast, Tommy?" croaked Tad, glugging a mouthful of fresh water.

"Leave it to me, I'll surprise you this time."

With that, Tommy jumped up and somersaulted away like a gymnast. Most impressive, thought Tad. What a terrific way to catch food, and show off.

"Bye-bye," he croaked, waving Tommy off again. "Come back safely."

Tommy stopped his acrobatics to shout back, "Thanks, Tad, you be careful too. Remember what I told you – stay safely in the hideout until I return. Won't be long."

"I'll make three froggy wishes. One for happiness, one for health and the other to be a big super-frog, like you."

Tommy chuckled as he leapt away. "At least two of those will come true, and quickly, young fella!"

Hearing that, Tad smiled and wondered, looking down

at his little body. He could not picture himself as a grown-up frog, but at least he was happy.

He sat motionless on the edge of the den, aware of what Tommy had told him. He had to be vigilant, especially with the likes of Fiona and Neville swirling around. They were always on the lookout for careless little tadpoles! Daydreaming about his brothers and sisters who had shared the jelly-ball with him, he wondered where they were right now.

The pond mist drifted slowly away as the sun climbed higher, then disappeared in a hurry as if sucked up by a vacuum cleaner. More creatures awoke, and Tad became scared. Where had Tommy got to? Although he had only been gone minutes in reality, it seemed like yonks. Being little, Tad thought time, like many things, was big and long.

"Wonder what the surprise breakfast will be. I'm more than a 'tad' hungry," he chuckled. "Teehee, my name means 'little'. It fits me perfectly at the moment."

Other country sounds and farmyard noises came to his ear from beyond where he was hiding. Schoolchildren were singing about an old farmer. Tad couldn't quite make out all the words, but it sounded cheerful and made him smile even more. It didn't even cross his mind to wonder why he, a tadpole, could understand the human song's words at all.

"Old MacDonald had a farm, Eee-i-eee-i-o…"

This was followed by a cheerful, soothing hymn about all things bright and beautiful, all creatures great and small, all things wise and wonderful, the Lord God made them all. The words grabbed him. He felt part of the song.

The children continued singing, and then Tad heard them greet the farmer, Frank. He wondered if Frank not only owned the farm, but Cloverdaisy Pond too. He wished he could get closer and have a look, but he decided to stay put where he was safe.

As the voices drifted away, a cuckoo called in the distance. Tad was enchanted by its repetitive, echoing cry, which sounded beautiful. However, Tommy had told him that the bird had a wicked reputation for stealing nests from other birds and throwing their eggs out – oh dear!

Feeling brave, Tad decided to drift to the surface. Turtledoves, very much in love, were cooing from the branches of an overhanging willow tree. Tad jumped as they suddenly flew off, wondering what had startled them. Just at that moment came another sound, one familiar to him.

Splish, splash, splosh, croak. Tommy, the crazy, lovable frog, had returned. His mouth was bursting with ready-scrunched beetles, horse flies and mosquitoes wrapped in a small acorn leaf – tasty and scrummy looking. He put the food down under one of his feet so it wouldn't fly off.

"Hey-up, Tommy, where d'ya get to? I've been very brave and heard many new sounds, especially country ones."

"Glad you are getting used to them, little fella, and sorry I was so long. Took a while to find a good feeding patch. Had to hop across more leaves than usual, but it does keep me fit. Here you go." Tommy laid out the mashed, tasty cuisine on a separate cloverleaf plate. "Tuck in, young Tad, it's lovely."

Tad did so with glee. Lost in the moment, they ate, but their concentration was lost too. Oh no!

Tad felt something nip the end of his tail. A large, angry fish had swum right up and taken a bite out of it – Fiona was on the hunt for unwary creatures! Tommy grabbed Tad swiftly in his mouth and whisked him straight back to the den below.

"Phew," he croaked. "That was a close shave. You OK, Tad?"

"Think so, Tommy, but the end of my bum feels funny, like it's stinging and buzzing."

Tommy glanced at Tad's tail. Although it was slightly shorter than before, there were no cuts or bruises, nor was it bleeding. How weird! However, it had also changed shape and colour.

"Look here, that pesky Fiona seems to have nipped the end of your tail off, but don't worry." Seeing Tad was about to cry, Tommy added, "There's no real injury. It's just a bit…well… er…it's like it has re-grown into something else, quickly. When they get to full size, frogs don't usually have a tail at all, nor do they need one for swimming, but with you, I'm not so sure…"

Tad was baffled by this. Why hadn't Tommy finished the sentence off properly? Did he realise something Tad didn't?

Tommy turned round so Tad could see his backend – there was no tail.

"See what I mean?"

"Wow!" exclaimed Tad. "Yes I do. Can't wait to look like that and be all grown-up."

"Don't wish your life away, young man," said Tommy, the elder frogs-man. "You will grow up soon enough. In fact, I have a strong intuition that you are to become very special…like the Chosen One!"

Tad pretended to look nonchalant. He'd thought he

was the only one who had any inkling about the strange power that seemed to have been bestowed on him from birth – the power he was slowly coming to realise. Life's journey had only just begun, but it was already surreal.

"Snap out of it, Tad," piped Tommy. "Have you eaten enough? Right, let's get that special tail exercised, make it more supple."

"What does that mean?" asked Tad.

"It means that if you wiggle the way I do, then you will feel stronger inside."

"Ooooh, I love the sound of that," Tad replied, getting ready to wiggle too.

"Up you go, stretch as far as you can, then wiggle all the way up and giggle all the way down."

Tad did indeed giggle as he thought the exercises were silly. His new tail, however, had a mind of its own.

Tommy continued more seriously. "To the left we go, to the right we row, as far as we can, stretch and throw. All the way, then bend like a bow and wiggle, wriggle, jiggle from side to side. Spin and leap and finish with a glide."

Even poetry thrown in. He must be crackers, thought Tad.

Before long, both of them were laughing so much that they fell in a heap.

"You're fine, Tad," croaked Tommy, relieved they had stopped. He couldn't keep up with the tadpole. "Your body strength and endurance are incredible for such a young frogling. So athletic, too."

"That's a new one," Tad mumbled under his breath. "A frogling?"

"You can even swim faster than I can. I followed you

quietly when you first hatched from the frogspawn, and even then I could not keep up with you."

Tad was chuffed to bits, over the moon – so much so

that he felt like jumping across the pond, but jumped high over Tommy instead.

"Fantastic," roared Tommy, not surprised at all at his friend's incredible agility. "You'll be all set for the Tad-pole-ympics at this rate!"

"What's the Tad-pole-ym…"

"Never mind that, we're off again now."

After settling Tad on his back, Tommy hopped over to a clearing in the pond. They looked up to see the hanging layered branches of the wonderful sixty-foot high weeping willow tree. The wind blew the leaves round like a carousel while they clung on tight, but the tree did not weep. No, it was far too happy for that. Tad saw in it a form of refuge and safety from the outside world, almost as if it were there to guard and protect them. It had enormous presence. Maybe, just maybe, protection would one day be exactly what they would need.

Tad shook his head, startled by the premonitions filling it. Then he pulled himself together and relaxed, remembering his resolution. Whatever happened, he would pull through it. He didn't know how he knew, but he knew he would.

After a brief interval, Tad and Tommy skipped off merrily again.

"Whoa," croaked Tommy in full cry as he squelched to a halt. "Look over there, mate."

Tad looked in shock. Flashes of dazzling bright white electric forks were stabbing the earth.

"That's called lightning. You'll hear a thunderclap soon… listen!"

Tad almost fainted with the loud bang that followed. Astonished, he reeled with awe and amazement at nature's

ferocity – a nature that he was a part of. At that moment, he felt like a very small creature in a big, big world.

After the lightning had struck and the thunder roared,

a colossal, heavy downpour of rain pelted the pond. The storm was of biblical proportions. It was time to find cover, quickly.

"Hang on tight," shouted Tommy. "Don't be frightened. The rain may push us under. Hold your breath if it does."

"I'm scared," shouted Tad under the tumult of rain. "I want my mum!"

The storm was relentless. Tad found that clinging to Tommy's back was getting harder and more slippery by the minute. Tommy understood why Tad was scared, but reminded him that he was almost fully grown. He had to be brave, storm or no storm.

"You'll be all right if you don't let go."

Tad looked at him pitifully, eyes brimming with tears. He knew his mum would not come, and Tommy would not be able to shield him from harm for ever.

The temperature plummeted and hailstones the size of marbles came down like bullets.

"Dive! Dive for cover, Tad, right now!" ordered Tommy. "The hailstones are deadly…"

Thud! Too late – Tad was hit, hard. Down into the depths of the pond he sank like a stone. Down, down and down until he could hear Tommy no more. He flipped and flapped to the surface, but the massive, pounding hailstones kept knocking him under.

"Get back up!" bawled Tommy, head held down in the water. Alas, he too was now in trouble, struggling to stay afloat. "Waggle your tail, Tad, hard. Make it buzz."

A miracle was needed, rapidly. It was the only thing that could save them now, but where, in their desperation, was it?

Three

To the Rescue

Slowly drowning, Tad desperately flung prayers into space and spun his tail…nothing. He was still not sure what would happen next, but faith told him to do it regardless.

He then heard the lovely words from his dream again, sung to the tune of a beautiful song:

"Long ago and far away,

I dreamed a dream one day."

The storm was raging furiously over the entire pond when suddenly, surging powerfully from the choppy waters like two otters, rose a pair of ginormous super-frogs. Grabbing Tad and Tommy from the deep, raging torrent and clamping each one tightly in their mouths, they swam to the bank. Jumping up through the branches of the special weeping willow to safety, the super-frogs placed Tad and Tommy on a hidden platform. Sanctuary – just as Tad had foretold.

"And now that dream is here beside me."

Tommy and Tad slept out the rest of the storm while their brave rescuers kept watch. These super-frogs had heard through the wireless frog-vine that a serious storm was afoot and all the pond life was in imminent danger of death. Acting swiftly and courageously, they had saved many lives already, before spotting Tommy and Tad drowning.

Still recovering from the drama, the two young frogs eventually opened their eyes and gasped. They were relieved and thrilled to see the two massive frogs peering at them.

"Who are you?" asked Tad.

The super-frogs glanced lovingly at each other and smiled.

"You know, don't you, Tommy?"

Tommy looked from one super-frog to the other and his eyes lit up.

"Mum! Dad!"

Tad gasped again.

"Yes, young Tad, we brought you into this world, and we want you to stay a bit longer. We are your parents, Mum and Dad – Albert and Victoria to our friends."

"Our parents?" Tommy quizzed in disbelief. "You mean we are related?"

"Yes, you are. What else? Nearly all the young frogs and tadpoles in Cloverdaisy are related in some way. We and your grandparents moved to a secret retirement pond many moons ago. However, we always return when the next generations are born. Cloverdaisy Pond was always a good place to start life in, but things are changing…"

"Wow!" said Tommy.

"We sensed the danger," explained Albert. "Besides, we heard young Jack, the farmer's son, talking about the mighty storm coming. Moreover, we felt the vibrations through Tad's tail from far away."

81

"Wow," croaked Tommy again, "incredible!" Tad was still stunned into silence. He'd thought what little he had done had not worked.

"Jack visits us in Frogstock Pond from time to time to see how everyone is doing. He's a saint, that lad. We all owe our lives to him and Frank, his dad, in many ways."

"Good gosh!" yelled Tad. "You mean that Frogstock Pond is real? I thought it only existed in my dreams."

"Yes, it is very real and special, just like you, Tad. That's where we heard young Jack talking. We thought it best to be near and help out if needed. Several frogs in our family have an amazing gift of speech and are able to converse with certain kind humans, like Jack."

"That's why I could understand the words that the schoolchildren were singing," said Tad excitedly. "I thought all frogs could understand humans."

Victoria tilted her head. "Oh no, Tad, not all frogs can do this, and hardly any frogs can do what you can do."

"What's that?"

"You'll find out in the fullness of time," said Victoria, half smiling. Then a sadness appeared in her large, bulbous eyes. "We have prophesied that an even greater tempest will destroy the whole of Cloverdaisy Pond, including you. Everyone must leave and travel across to Frogstock. Property developers will eventually take over the remains and build houses here."

Tad and Tommy went white with shock, then anger took over. They had already come to love their comfortable home and surroundings, but were now being challenged to leave.

"How can we move out, it's all we have?" asked Tommy, feeling quite sick and sad at the very thought, let alone the threat.

"Frank the local farmer will help out and do much of the hard graft. He, Jack and the rest of the farm-hands will divert some of this pond across to the small duck lake by the farm. This will act as an overflow for any creatures too old or young or sick to travel. But you cannot use this diversion as an escape route. It is too small, and it has no link to Frogstock Pond. The huge surface water pipe at the south end of the pond will be your exit. It is the only one large enough to take you all. Timing will be critical. A lull will develop when the sun shines continually for sixteen hours at the end of the month. When the sun stops shining, that will be your cue to move. Tad will know."

The two brothers were dead silent. It was too much to take in, but the situation was critical – a life or death scenario would unfurl, then what? Presumably they'd swim or float away. More importantly, how?

"Right, dear children, we must leave now," said Albert. "It's much warmer over at Frogstock Pond and we cannot stand the cold for too long. Underground hot water springs keep the water tepid so species from warmer climates can survive and breed there too. It never freezes. We look forward to you joining us. Keep safe but be strong."

"If you accomplish your mission," added Victoria, "we will all have more time together. As a further precaution, there is a small secret pipe that leads right through to the pond if you cannot get down the main tunnel. It is only big enough for two frogs at a time and can be found by the abandoned foxhole. There is also a pipe back to the farm aquarium, if anyone needs urgent medical help or super heat. That lies behind the willow tree in a maze of bramble – only our kind can get to it. Apart from Jack, no one else knows about these tunnels, not even predators, so they're quite safe. Look out for the Messengers."

"Messengers, what messengers?" asked Tommy. "Is that a riddle?"

There was no reply. Both parents had disappeared back to their beloved Frogstock Pond, leaving a thin vapour trail. A few seconds later, it had changed colour to a tiny rainbow.

Tad hung his head, then lifted it back to the skies in joy, whispering, "Magic, pure magic. Thank you for coming."

Tommy was caught in the moment too. "Look again, Tad, an even larger rainbow now, and it's touching you! There's something in this. It's like a sign, an omen – mystical, little brother, mystical." He then remembered a phrase he'd heard the school kids recite to help them remember the rainbow's colours. "Richard Of York Gave Battle In Vain – Red, Orange, Yellow, Green, Blue, Indigo and Violet."

"You are most wise, Tommy, but there are many things I still don't understand, yet I can feel them."

"Neither do I, little fella, but we both will in time."

The rain stopped as quickly as it had started and out came the sun, shining brightly. A herd of beautiful black and white cows came over to drink rainwater that had formed puddles by the side of the pond.

"Those are Cloverdaisy's Friesian cows," said Tommy. "The farmer gets milk from them which people have on their breakfast cereal and in cups of tea."

"Ooooooh," said Tad, feeling honoured that the cows had come to visit the pond. "But why are they freezing? It's such a lovely, warm day now."

"Freezing?" asked Tommy, puzzled. Then he laughed, realising Tad had misheard him. "They are Friesian cows,

Tad. That's their breed. They're not freezing, silly thing. There are other breeds too, but Friesians are best for milk."

Both giggled.

"Right, we are safe for the moment, but we mustn't forget the warnings our parents gave when they left. There will be Nevilles and Fionas everywhere now, so be careful. Let's crack on with the rescue mission. We need to get our brothers, sisters, cousins and the rest of the pond life together for a team meeting and prepare an escape."

"Look over yonder," interrupted Tad. "Children coming."

"Quick, here, get well back and pose on this lily like a model. The kids will take their socks and shoes off to paddle over and take photographs for their nature album. That's how they learn about pond and animal life."

Tad did as Tommy asked, even though he was nervous. He had never had his photograph taken before – whatever that was.

As it happened, water levels were too high from the storm for the children to paddle. Instead, they took photographs from the side of the pond before throwing bread in for the eider ducks, Canadian geese and herring gulls that had assembled. The geese would be migrating soon.

After they had gone, Tad Pole and Tommy Frog played peek-a-boo with one another through the reeds and leaves, performing acrobatics in the clear, fresh rainwater, stopping only to catch their breath. They then heard a "Baaaahhhhh" – a flock of sheep and their lambs had come to greet them.

Tad stared, smiling yet amazed at the playful lambs and their sensible mothers. Tommy explained, "The older sheep grow wool for clothing which the farmer shears off. That's what the kids sometimes call their annual haircuts. He also milks them and turns it into cheese and butter, just like he does with the cows. He does the same with the goats."

On hearing this, Billy, the mad goat, came clattering over to see what was going on. He was the mascot for the local brass band, and very nosey. He also had horns like baby elephant tusks, which frightened Tad.

"Watch him," shouted Tommy. "He can be nasty with those horns if you upset him. He charged at Jack the other day and clipped him up the backside – painfully! Jack couldn't sit down for days."

How funny, but oh dear, thought Tad, relieved when Billy eventually moved off to a far corner. "Tom-meee," he said, thoughtfully, "why don't the sheep get cold? They must be freezing like the cows when they have no coats on."

"The sheep only have their wool clipped in summer when it's warm. It grows back for the winter. They are lucky. If the farmer didn't clip them, they'd overheat and struggle to breathe. Flies would lay eggs in their wool, which hatch as maggots, causing them great distress. Urrguurrrhh! You should see the cardigans and coats that the wool makes once it's woven into fabric. Gorgeous, and very warm, of course."

Next, a whirring and buzzing sound came close. It frightened Tad a bit. "Get away, you funny thing, leave me alone!" His arms were so little that he could not shoo it off properly.

"It's a dragonfly, it won't harm you," said Tommy. "Fortunately you're too big now, but they do eat baby tadpoles."

"What a close shave, then," muttered Tad. "But what lovely, bright, shining colours."

"Certainly are," replied Tommy. "Blue, black and grey with two sets of silver shimmering wings. The species is over 300 million years old and can fly backwards or forwards up to twenty miles per hour, or simply hover like a hummingbird. They also eat loads of insects, like we do. Remind me of old-fashioned model aeroplanes. They drone like them too!"

Tad half smiled, still uncomfortable. He was thinking of food again, and Tommy could sense this. Even Tommy was getting peckish.

"Look over there, more guests in our pond: the Royal Swans, and their young which are called cygnets. They're protected by the Queen's Charter. This means that the Queen has a right of ownership over all swans in our village and the whole of the country…"

Tad looked puzzled again. "What's a queen?" he asked.

"The Queen is the ruler of our country, England."

"Wow!" Tad replied, puffing his tiny chest out and feeling quite proud. "It's great to be living in a country with a Queen at the head. Is she like our mum? Wise and magical too?"

"She is indeed, though she's not a Frog Queen. She's human, just like the grown-ups and children we've seen today. I'm sure she also loves frogs, tadpoles and all the other creatures that live here."

Along they went, piggybacking and leap frogging as if on an obstacle course, seeing who could jump higher or swim faster. Tad won every time by a mile. As the weeks passed, they played like this for hours, having a good time, eating, drinking and talking about their parents and survival.

Eventually Tad, exhausted from all the over-activity, dozed off. Tommy towed him along to an empty, warm, snug and cosy duck's nest, then nodded off too.

Tad woke up with a start. He felt he had slept the clock round – and, in fact, he had. Several times. A whole week had passed. Something had happened…

Four

During the deep sleep, Tad's arms and legs had changed. His body had filled out too, despite his not having eaten, and he had become a greeny-gold colour. Surprisingly, he still had the semblance of a tail, which now looked like a rainbow coloured ice cream cone. How bizarre!

One thing was certain: he was now a fully-grown frog, just like his older brother, but even bigger. Tommy was loath to tell him. He wanted it to be a surprise, so he perched Tad on the edge of the nest.

"Look, Tad, see any difference? Watch when the water ripples. See how it bends and bows, changing how our reflections look on the surface. You're more than fully grown…sheesh!"

Tad peeped at his reflection, which made him jump. "Wow!" he croaked. His voice was a bit deeper than it had been before, but it was the change in his colour, shape and size that foxed him. "It's nice of you to say, Tommy, but I loved being tiny. It was short, sweet and friendly."

"Look again as the fish jump and splash, making us wibbly-wobbly even though we're not moving. And when we stand together, it's like I'm almost seeing my double, but that tail of yours is…well, that's something else. Quite unique."

"Ha-ha, we shall see. I will be thrilled just to hop around with you and see if you can still keep up."

Tommy blushed. "Thanks, brother. I will try, but you will be able to do even more now."

Suddenly Tommy felt giddy and quivered, while Tad went into a trance as if hypnotised. They knew the time their parents had warned them about was drawing near and they could no longer delay the plans. Quickly snapping out of the spell, Tommy continued the conversation.

"We've come a long way. However, a colossal amount of work is needed for our mission to succeed. Once we're at Frogstock, we can live safely again and have families of our own."

"You're right," replied Tad. "Mum and Dad will be thrilled to see us, if we make it. I will be sad to say goodbye to Cloverdaisy, but I am looking forward to the challenge."

"I too will be sad, but we will make it. Well, you will make it, of that I'm sure. It's where your destiny lies. Here's to the future!"

Despite their doubt and uncertainty, both frogs were happy with the plans they had in mind.

Night time fell again quickly so they ate early and bedded down in their den. Work would start at dawn – a fresh start.

*

Mid-way through his sleep, Tommy suddenly shot up and nudged Tad. He vaguely remembered something about when they were drowning, before their mum and dad had appeared.

"Hey," he whispered, "I think I may have seen some giant bullfrog cousins of ours when we were sinking during the storm. I read about them in *Frog Weekly*. They are very famous and carry out dangerous rescue missions, like the SAS – 'Who Dares Wins'."

"No-oooo," muttered Tad, yawning. "Go back to sleep, it's too early."

Tommy wouldn't listen and continued excitedly, "If it was them, they would make superb bodyguards. They're huge, ferocious, strong and fearless. They normally live in much warmer waters, but they are the only others who could possibly know of our plight – the wireless frog-vine again!" He looked at the starlight then across the top of the pond…nothing! However, he knew he had not hallucinated.

Tad shrugged him off, saying, "It's a fantasy, Tom, a dream. Get some sleep!"

He had spoken too soon, though. Something was stirring.

"Look, Tad!" whispered Tommy, wide awake. "I think we might need bodyguards now, not just later!"

Huge, bright, bulging radar eyes surged menacingly towards them.

"W-h-a-t are they?" shrieked Tad, trembling and wishing he was still tiny enough to hide. Puffing his chest out fearlessly, he tried to look like Hercules, but gave up quickly and dived for cover.

As he did so, three torpedo-shaped missiles-with-legs burst through the pond's surface like submarine rockets. Huge frogs, the largest on God's earth, with mouths like giant lizards and feet like komodo dragons, they had awesome presence. Tad was thunderstruck; Tommy was lost for words.

"I am, errr, we are very pleased to meet you, whopping giants," said Tad.

Silence. It was scary. They were incredible hulks, massive bullfrogs, monsters of the deep. Then they croaked, though it sounded more like a cannon booming.

"We were listening a while back. You were not seeing things during the hailstorm, Tommy. Victoria and Albert, our cousins – your mum and dad – got in touch. They knew extra help was needed, quickly! Your parents, their ancestors and Jack's family up at the farm saved us from extinction light years ago – they are all fine folk and good frog people, the very best. We are the designated 'Froddy' Guards, the Am-Phib-Ian Army. I am Am, this is Phib, and the quiet one is Ian."

Tommy burst in to introduce himself and Tad. "Pleased to meet you all." They shook hands as the greetings continued. Ian nodded and stepped back. He seemed shy at being singled out, even though he had muscles like Superman and eyes brighter than diamonds. He was clearly not to be underestimated.

Tad felt him out telepathically, and Ian replied in the same way. Something special here, Tad thought.

An uncomfortable but respectful silence followed after the last Froddy Guard had spoken. Tad whispered to Tommy, who then said, "You seem incredible, but my brother reckons the water is too cold for you here." Tommy was quivering with fright, but inside he was leaping with joy at the unexpected arrivals and their size.

Am, who was obviously the ring leader, replied, "You guessed correctly, cousins."

Oooh, cousins, thought Tad. Comforting.

"We have access to even deeper hot water springs beneath the pond and recharge our body heat down there. We also have a path to the secret sub-channel pipes that link us to Frogstock Pond and Jack's warm aquarium tank at the farm. No one else is aware, except a chosen few... and your parents, of course. Geddit?"

"Yes!" Tad and Tommy were both proud to hear that their parents were involved.

Phib continued, "We originally came from a place called the United States of America. Our species was in grave danger of becoming extinct there. Kind-hearted animal lovers arranged for us to emigrate on a boat to your country and live in a zoo."

Tad and Tommy looked aghast as Am carried on from Phib.

"However, we felt like prisoners – trapped. We like to swim and roam around in peace and freedom, so we decided to escape, but we were not sure how to do it. Purely by chance, when Jack came to the docks to collect other rare amphibians for his breeding programme, he noticed we were distressed. He managed to swap our tank with one of the other large fish tanks on the harbour side without anyone seeing. He got quite a shock when he opened the tank and realised just how big we are, and that he could talk to us, but still he took us home to his farm. We were made so welcome."

"We understand humans too…" began Tad, but Tommy stopped him, keen to hear more about the life of a giant bullfrog.

"Thing is," said Ian, floating quietly and flexing his body, "we are glad to be alive and enjoy being liberated. We want the same for all of you."

"Right, that's enough of the intros," said Tommy, licking his blubbery lips. "We are hungry. No doubt you are too, so why not join us for breakfast?"

Am looked at Phib, and Phib looked at Ian, and Ian looked at Am. As one, they all nodded then boomed, "Yeah!"

"Good, that settles it," said Tommy, delighted to have their company. "Er…what shall we eat? Haven't got anything in."

"Don't worry, we'll catch it," said Am, setting off with the other pair in tow. Moments later, much to Tommy and Tad's great excitement, they returned, mouths stuffed with fruit flies, grubs and all manner of crunchy creepy-crawlies. A banquet!

After the finest feast of a breakfast that Cloverdaisy had ever produced, Phib made an announcement.

"Be on your guard at all times. Be vigilant! Predators are everywhere."

Tad and Tommy, wide-eyed, nodded approvingly, glad of the reminder.

"Just as importantly," Am added, "we must focus seriously on the second almighty storm that is coming. The escape plan must be ready for when it does. Your parents have told us the bulls are coming too – not handsome bullfrogs like us, nor male cows, but mechanical bulldozers. They will dig out and drain the remains of the pond once the floods recede. Sadly, any remaining life will be destroyed. The storm will arrive soon, but only one among us knows exactly when."

Their eyes all zoomed in on Tad. He looked away diffidently.

"Yes, I feel that too," said Tommy. "It's a spiritual thread we all possess – a natural awareness, like knowing how to catch flies. We can all sense danger."

Lost in the moment, none of the frogs visibly realised the immediate danger lurking a few inches away. Ferocious Fiona the Giant Carp and Neville the Nasty Newt had been eavesdropping on their conversation, listening furtively with great interest.

Fiona whispered to Neville, "Maybe we should make a pact and escape together."

Bang! They'd been overheard. In a flash, Ian and Phib had snapped both up in their jaws as if they were going to eat them whole.

"You two, over here!" roared Am. "Spying, were you? Treachery, eh? Well, you are hostages now while we decide what to do with you."

Tommy and Tad, although scared, were impressed. It had happened so quickly – like lightning.

"Put them in the cage, brothers," growled Am, gesturing towards a high-security cage anchored below the pond's surface. "We made it yesterday, cousins, knowing enemies like these would be lurking surreptitiously. It's a prison made from wire, hawthorn and fish bone spikes."

After frog-marching Fiona and Neville in, Ian bound their tails, Neville's feet and Fiona's fins with reed cuffs. Frightened to death by the arrest, they were silent, as if they'd lost their tongues. As Ian and Phib swished the bandits to the back of the makeshift prison, Tad and Tommy peered into the cage, relieved they had been caught.

"Keep watch in turns," ordered Am as he swam off with Phib and Ian, staring intimidatingly at the prisoners as he went as if to say, "Don't move. Don't even think about it!"

The young frogs thanked the Froddy Guards humbly, realising how lucky they had been. Having the Froddy Guards on board now would be a great advantage. It was clear the entire mission would be a team effort, not an individual one.

Tad was so thrilled that he jumped on to one of the clumps and burst into song:

I am H.A.P.P.Y.,
I am H.A.P.P.Y.,
I know I am, I'm sure I am,
I am H.A.P.P.Y…

Tad was interrupted by loud applause. He looked around, surprised – the rest of the pond life had surfaced in a glossy shoal to join in with the next verse. It was quite a spectacle, and brought tears to his tiny binocular eyes; to think this could be the last time Cloverdaisy Pond enjoyed a moment of such pure joy.

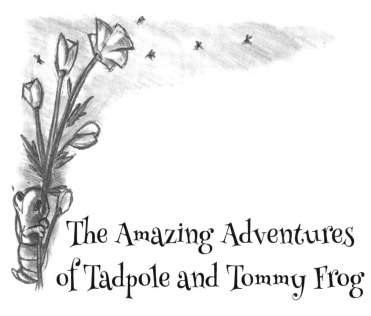

The Amazing Adventures of Tadpole and Tommy Frog

Part Two – The Tragedy of Cloverdaisy Pond

One

Warnings

Above the pond, the heat of the day had drained Tad and Tommy. It was time for a nap. Neville and Fiona, too frightened to sleep, had noticed that the frogs were taking a break so they started whispering again about an escape…

Wuumph!

"Don't even think about it," bellowed Am. The three Froddy Guards had returned early to relieve their cousins of sentry duty. Staring menacingly at the prisoners, they threw some food down. Neville and Fiona were grateful to have something to eat, if nothing else.

The bullfrogs got ready to leave again. "Where are you off to now?" asked Tommy, yawning like a hippo.

"They need warmth quickly, so they are heading back to the heated aquarium at the farm," replied Tad. Tommy looked baffled, and even two of the Froddy Guards looked surprised that Tad had guessed their intentions so accurately, but Ian nodded wisely. He wasn't much of a talker, but he had strong telepathic connections with Tad and had communicated a psychic message while Am and Phib were dealing with Fiona and Neville.

"Keep an eye on the prisoners," he said, out loud this time for the benefit of the others. "They are quite devious. As a precaution, we will send three more surprises. You will like them."

When they had gone, Tommy invited the rest of the pond life to hear the escape plans. Word was spreading fast and the other inhabitants were getting nervous.

"I'll climb up the poker-shaped reeds and ring the buttercup bells to alert everyone," croaked Tad. He shimmied to the top where he swished and swayed in the breeze like a pole-vaulter who had forgotten to let go.

"Oyez, oyez, hear this, here this! Listen closely, all of you."

Everyone gathered quickly.

"Soon a ferocious storm, the worst ever, will hit us hard… very hard. We must prepare to escape to our new home at Frogstock Pond. Help will be on hand to assist. You will have seen the giant American bullfrogs gliding around earlier – they are not just friends and allies, but our cousins too. Don't be frightened, they will not harm you."

There were gasps of astonishment as everyone listened intently.

"Firstly, trust us. Do you understand?"

Everyone nodded.

"Under no circumstances are you to panic when the

rains come, otherwise we could all drown before we even start." Tad then boomed the biggest declaration of his entire life. "Success is not final, failure is not fatal – it is the courage to continue that counts. Remember that and keep it in your hearts."

The wisdom and seriousness of what Tad had just said hit home. Some of the Cloverdaisy Pond inhabitants sobbed, others felt inspired by the command.

Full of emotion himself, Tommy then addressed the pack in small groups to allay further fears. There was quite a mix – Blanche Blue Tit and her family, Biddy Blackbird and her clan, together with Flo and the finches, the Quackle Ducks and their quacklings, Mrs Thrush and her thrushettes, Walt and his formation wagtail dancing team, Victor and Vera the grass voles, Martha and her musical mouselettes, Sid and Sophie Swan and their cygnets, Betty Beaver and her dam builders, Willy and his wily water boatman, Terence Tadpole and his tribe, Lord Frederick Frog and his minions. In fact, just about everyone who lived in Cloverdaisy Pond, including those who did not have such silly names, listened keenly to the escape plan before leaving to prepare their own life craft. Some treated it like an adventure, quite relaxed, while others dreaded the prospect. They all liked the sound of Frogstock Pond, but wondered if such a dangerous mission could be accomplished. It sounded far too treacherous for such vulnerable, delicate creatures. They would need faith by the bucket loads, and with it would come hope.

Tad eventually slid down the stem of the reed and hugged as many animals as he could. Am, Phib and Ian

returned, well fed and happy to have warmed up again.

"No surprises yet?" asked Am.

"No, haven't seen any," said Tad.

As Tad and Tommy approached the main HQ platform they'd created in the middle of the pond for a leadership meeting with the Froddy Guards, something was shadowing them like a ghostly silhouette. The next moment, three enormous furry bodies erupted from the water and landed abruptly right beside the five leader frogs. Their sheer size and presence was phenomenal. As big as otters with tails like giant iguanas, they had enormous razor-sharp front teeth that flashed like white piano keys, shining so brightly they dazzled everyone. What was really mesmerising, though, was their speed through the water, as if powered by jets.

They introduced themselves as Raj, Saj and Taj, the mighty Indian water voles. The surprise had now arrived.

Tad, completely speechless, nudged Tommy, who couldn't believe his eyes either. Phib spoke first.

"These guys live with us at the aquarium. They originally sneaked on board a merchant ship carrying endangered species from India."

Raj took up the story. "We were fortunate to escape from the harbour like the bullfrogs did. It was all down to Jack. Thankfully, he spotted us down the side of an embankment. We'd come from an upturned cargo lorry, which had rolled off the landing platform. We were not hurt, but needed water quickly. Several of our brethren, sadly, got crushed to death.

"We thrive on adventure just like the Froddy Guards, and try to help others whose survival is threatened. Am explained what you are doing, which moved us. Occasionally, we and the Froddy Guards swim the hidden pipe channel to Frogstock Pond and visit our cousins there. However, we cannot stay too long as it is not warm enough for us survive there, despite the hot underground springs. We are warriors, but are friendly and on good terms with everyone at the aquarium and Frogstock Pond."

The trio was warmly received and treated to honey tea, watercress sandwiches and clover cream for dessert. They had voracious appetites so tucked in wholeheartedly.

Afterwards, Tad and Tommy headed back to their lily beds for sleep. Soon the pond was quiet and peaceful as the inhabitants got some much needed rest. Only Fiona and Neville remained wide awake, ever watchful for a chance to escape.

Silence reigned over the pond until dawn when Jack strolled across the meadow to collect the cows for milking. As he did so, he sang one of his favourite songs:

"Morning has broken, like the first morning,
Blackbird has spoken, like the first bird.
Praise for the singing, praise for the morning,
Praise for the springing fresh from the word."

Tad and Tommy woke to the sweet chorus. It was lovely. They were used to the many sounds of the pond and were suddenly reluctant to leave, but leave they must, and soon.

The order of the day was set by Fiona the No Longer Ferocious asking if she and Neville could be let out of the cage. Although imprisoned in the water, they too needed to leave at some point; worried that their own kindred would be left at the mercy of the bulldozers. When the Froddy Guards returned, Phib hopped over and asked them some questions.

"Right, you pair, spill the beans. What were you doing yesterday sneaking around? What's this about wanting to be let out?"

Scared witless and quivering, Neville replied, "We heard

your escape plans. We do not want to drown either, or get bull-charged…"

"Bull-charged?" roared Phib. "You mean bulldozed, stupid nit. People are going to build here!"

"Sorry, that's what we meant. We have families too. We cannot think straight at the moment, we are too frightened, what with you locking us in here and that storm coming…"

"So you should be," Phib growled. "Don't tell lies, though – you were spying for the herons, weren't you?"

"No, not at all…"

"Don't answer back. Shut up and listen," snapped Ian.

Fiona, holding tears back, said, "Yes, you are right. They said they'd eat us if we didn't, but we now see no sense in spying. It's far more important that we protect our own species otherwise the pond life will have no ecological balance. Please forgive us and grant our release. We can make a real contribution to the rescue plan, and…"

"That's probably true," Tad butted in, "but how can we trust a pair of sneaks like you?"

"Call it a pact," replied Neville. "We can be friends until we all get to Frogstock Pond and then go our separate ways, let nature take its course. What do you say to that?"

The five frogs and three Indian voles grouped together in a circle, shaking their heads and nodding until they came to a decision. Tommy was spokes-frog.

"We have agreed to release you on one condition."

Fiona and Neville widened their eyes and held their breath.

"You harm no one and leave us in peace, except when we need to liaise with each other about the rescue plan.

When, not if, we get to the new pond, you must keep to your own quarter, well away from ours, or else. We have always been natural enemies, but this is our one opportunity to work together to survive and maybe, just maybe, live in some sort of future harmony. What do you say?"

Tommy finished his ultimatum then backed away, giving the captives a moment to themselves. The pressure was intense. There was really only one choice…no choice!

After embracing Neville and nodding, Fiona turned and spoke.

"Yes, it's a deal." Then she thanked the committee for sparing their lives. However, she and Neville were under strict orders to avoid any trickery or deceit, and they would be supervised at all times. If there was any double-crossing or shenanigans, they would be imprisoned again and left to perish.

Finally the escape plans started in earnest. After each frenetic day's labour at Cloverdaisy Pond, the work gangs could hardly believe it was nightfall again. Supper filled their bellies and sleep filled their minds. In no time at all, rich, croaky, warbly snores rang through the misty night air, interrupted only by the occasional owl or barking-mad fox.

The inseparable duo of Tommy and Tad were first to roll out of bed each morning, shaking their heads in the water to refresh themselves then thinking about the imminent danger. Tad knew that if the storm didn't get them, unseen predators or humans probably would.

Are we ever going to be safe? he thought, giving Tommy a reassuring hug in the process.

Some of the other creatures were dreaming of a new life to come, while the pessimists remained doubtful. But despite the many obstacles, they needed to finish all the life craft in double quick time. Putting their fears aside, they caught and dished up a variety of breakfasts in style. Neville, Fiona and their families were allowed to join them at a safe distance, while the Froddy Guards kept a close eye on them just in case.

Tad meditated, thinking over the whole situation and how it had brought them together with their enemies, just like the dream he'd had about Frogstock Pond when he was a tadpole. He realised natural instincts and desires could be checked not just for the common good, but for survival too. After breakfast, he withdrew to a quiet corner and pondered the future. He could sense a change in the air, and had a sudden premonition about a single bright star appearing in the sky just before the storm arrived. His psychic senses told him that this would be the sign – their cue to take cover and get ready to leave.

Two

Storm Clouds Gather

During the many days of hard graft, Tommy had often noticed Tad sidling off to the south side of the pond where the tunnel was, so he decided to join him one day to see what was going on. In silence, they both sat and prayed before Tommy, concerned, asked Tad what was troubling him.

"I'm troubled by who will survive and who won't. I know I'm a so-called 'big boy' now, but I'm nervous like everyone else. What will happen when we escape?"

"That's out of our hands, dear Tad. We can only do our best."

Comforted and more at ease, Tad decided to confide in Tommy about his premonition.

"How can you know? Is that possible? Can you foretell the future?" Tommy asked in awe.

"Our parents passed the gift on to me during the spawn.

Remember, I dreamed of Frogstock Pond before I even knew it existed? Only a select few of our species are born with the special genes. We are chosen by a power beyond this world and are truly blessed. It is something we cherish and have a duty to use for the good of all animal kind. I may be the only one who survived out of over five thousand tadpoles. Only the Frog Gods know."

Tommy nodded. "Yes, I know."

"We are the lucky ones."

"I prefer fortunate to lucky," said Tommy. "It's tough, but true. We have so many enemies out there that life does not get any easier, even when we grow. We must keep focused and watch out for one another, and everyone else we love. This is the essence of life."

"It is, Tommy, and there's no time to lose. Tell them all."

Back at Cloverdaisy Pond, Tommy climbed up the same reed that Tad had used days earlier and cleared his throat. Croaking at the top of his voice, he summoned all the pond life and announced the news.

"OK, everyone, we must now go up a gear and work faster. We have fewer than twenty-four hours left to complete our tasks. The storm is approaching, so knuckle down and be ready. Good luck – give it your very best shot, and God speed."

Applause thundered from all sides of the pond following Tommy's rallying cry. In fact, it was so loud that Frank the farmer came over to see what the fuss was about. As he stared across, the giant bullfrogs and Indian water voles darted into the reeds – they must not be seen otherwise the farmer would know they had broken out of the aquarium and take them straight back for safety. Then the escape plan could fail.

After a few moments, the coast was clear again and a frenzy of work started in earnest. The exertions lasted well into the night. Nothing was left to chance – nothing that would jeopardise the mission. Each tribe did its best to work alongside one another, and jobs were allocated to families and teams according to individual skills. The entire pond was like a vast aquatic workshop.

Life rafts were made from twigs, tied together with reed heads to make them buoyant. Abandoned swan and duck nests were gathered to make boats and lined with discarded polythene bags to stop them sinking. Large fresh oak tree leaves were woven with small pieces of baling twine and bound to discarded bamboo sticks to act as canoes. However, Tommy kept the smaller oak leaves for himself, which puzzled Tad and the Froddy Guards somewhat.

Dinghies were carved from empty plastic bottles, while willow and bracken were fixed to the sides as ladders, making it easier to climb on board. A lot of useful debris was retrieved and recycled from the choked entrance to the tunnel. This exercise served a dual purpose as it would help surge the floodwater more rapidly and get them to the other side quickly. Nothing must block its flow.

Tad, Tommy, the Froddy Guards and water voles concentrated all their skills on making life jackets for the tiddly creatures. These were assembled from old toothpaste tubes filled with air and tied together with reed stalks. As for the fresh frogspawn, they were fortunate. The jelly-ball wrapped tightly around them would bounce and bob along like a giant float.

The final morning dawned at Cloverdaisy Pond. The last of the work continued with all the inhabitants more positive and upbeat about the journey than they'd ever been. It would be tough for sure, but there was only one alternative – death.

During lunch, Tommy whispered to Tad that he and the Froddy Guards had devised a separate plan. The frogs would set all the Fionas and Nevilles at the front of the evacuation queue to watch them properly as they went down the tunnel. Better still, being large, they could shunt any remaining debris that was blocking it.

"Great idea!" declared Tad, even though it sounded a bit like they were going to be used as battering rams.

After eating, all the groups worked flat out on their tasks. Dusk fell earlier than before, signalling that the lull Tad and Tommy's parents had spoken of, when the sun shone for sixteen hours a day, had passed. The days were getting shorter and Cloverdaisy Pond was about to get smaller.

Tad gazed at the night sky, which had cleared to reveal hundreds of stars. Farmer Frank had completed the afternoon milking much earlier, but did not turn the cows out again that night. His behaviour told Tad that he also knew something. Eerily, the birdsong had stopped too. No noise came from either the farmyard or the woods beyond. A sombre, sinister atmosphere pervaded the whole enclave – the proverbial calm before the storm.

A cool, misty night air shrouded the pond. This was the last time it would ever look like this. Tad knew the time had almost come. He gazed in a mystical trance, his eyes barely open. The stars were shining extremely bright as he'd predicted, still it was the not the sign he was looking for...yet.

Tommy checked that the life craft were ready and anchored. "What is it, Tad?" he quizzed.

Before Tad could reply, the entire pond turned pitch black. Tad gawped, open mouthed, while Tommy just stared. There it was – one star remaining, the shiniest he had ever seen. Sirius, the brightest star in the solar system, was the sign. Tad knew the hour had come.

Time was of the essence. It was ten o'clock already and most of the pond life had settled down for the night. Tad and Tommy rallied the Mighty Six – the Froddy Guards and the Indian water voles – together and told them of his prophecy. No one doubted his sincerity or truth; they had felt all along there was something eldritch about this peculiar little creature.

Gathering in a circular hug, solemn and spiritual, the eight of them bowed their heads and meditated for motivation. Breaking quickly from the embrace, they then woke every one up. Many were nervous and frightened as they ate at Cloverdaisy Pond for the last time, while others pretended to laugh it off, hoping this would calm their nerves.

The storm was close at hand. It would soon hit with tremendous force. The taller frogs had already seen the lightning and could hear the thunder getting closer. It was coming with a vengeance.

"Take to your stations, everyone," hollered Tommy. "Get

down to the bed. Tie all the little ones to the anchor rope. Hold on tightly – it's fixed to the bottom. Try to breathe when you get the chance or whenever the waves break. Tad says the storm will last for hours and will flood the entire pond and surrounding fields, over twenty feet deep. Do not untie the rope unless you need more air from the top, otherwise the breakers will sweep you away. Stay calm. Think of the new life at Frogstock Pond – our family and friends will be there waiting for us."

As Tommy finished his war cry, forks of lightning flashed overhead, followed immediately by fierce thunderclaps which shook the entire pond. The storm had begun right on cue, just as Tad had foretold. Seconds later the lightning struck again, shooting like laser beams, slicing everything in its path. Several trees by the edge of the pond took the full impact, crashing down into the water. Anything underneath was destroyed instantly, but things were about to get worse.

Tad, Tommy and the Mighty Six kept a sturdy command and blurry watch from the HQ platform in the middle of the pond. Despite being firmly tied, it was ducking and bobbing like a fisherman's boat at sea as they held on tight. Debris swirled everywhere in the wash; visibility was virtually nil. However, the leaders' acute radar hearing and Tad's psychic senses helped them navigate the carnage. There were few reported casualties…so far.

The storm raged well into the night as if possessed by the devil. Everyone hung on for grim death, but gripped even harder to survive. No one wanted to die. All they could do was hope and pray.

*

After nine hours of torrential rain, many creatures had perished. The floodwater was too deep for the smaller ones to swim up for air.

Seeing the struggle going on around him, Tommy realised he could wait no longer and revealed his reason for stashing the smaller oak leaves. He had devised an ingenious method of trapping air in the leaf parcels before sewing them up. They would act like the oxygen bottles that scuba divers wear on their backs to breathe underwater. Tommy had planted all of them along the bed of the pond when the level was much lower – how hard that must have been. He'd waited for as long as he could before using them, as the air supply would soon run out. Now it was time to play his hand.

After much croaking, huffing and puffing, Tommy released hundreds of water snails with a hidden lever from where they had been attached to the bottom of the pond using suction, holding the air parcels in place. Tiny reed tubes were strapped to the parcels' sides through which the air could be sucked. Many of the tiddly creatures managed to grab one, gasping for breath as they ran out of oxygen.

Everyone, including the giant bullfrogs and water voles, were astonished at Tommy's ingenuity and courage – what an amazing invention! Even Tad proudly gave his efforts the thumbs up.

"But how," Am wondered, "did you keep them on the bottom for so long?"

Tad overheard and pointed to all the water snails drifting on top of the pond where they were trying to keep stragglers afloat.

"Our secret weapon against the storm," shouted Tommy. "They didn't mind helping – they are incredible little fellows. They can cling to the pond bed like limpets – nothing can shift 'em, not even the strongest currents. I connected them to a life rope made from a ball of baling twine left on the bank. As soon as they felt me tug it, they released the parcels and floated up with them."

"Wow, that's incredible, you deserve a medal!"

The storm was relentless. After pounding and raging for over twelve hours, its ferocity finally began to wane. Tad and the other leaders dived to the bottom to check the harnesses were all still secure. They did not need extra air – all had incredible lungpower and swimming strength. Strangely, though, Tommy was not with them.

Tad found him…at the bottom, trapped and motionless, and distraught. He shook Tommy's arm – nothing. No movement, only silence.

He then noticed a thin trail of blood seeping from Tommy's ears and looked closer. Tommy had taken a huge blow to the head and was unconscious, and drowning.

"Tommy, Tommy," he bubbled and glugged, shaking his brother violently to stir him. Still nothing. Something was seriously wrong.

Sealing his lips over Tommy's, Tad blew strongly, as if trying to blow a candle out. Hundreds of star shaped bubbles swirled from his mouth and nostrils, circling Tommy's head before passing through his ears and drifting to the surface. Tommy's body followed.

Drained but calm now, Tad summoned Ian over telepathically. Sensing tragedy, all of the Big Six had been watching Tad closely and had just witnessed something extraordinary. As soon as Ian heard Tad's frantic call in his head, he swam swiftly to his friend's side followed by Am, Phib and the water voles. They were all fearing the worst, until…

Tommy started to groan a bit and blow bubbles. He was still alive! Tad knew already, of course – he had made sure of that.

"Hang on, big brother, we'll soon get you up. Come on, fellas," he added to Raj, Taj and Saj. "Give us a lift, he's badly hurt."

There was no hesitation. Despite the inclement weather and strong undercurrent, the Indian water voles and Tad stretchered Tommy to the bank. He groaned, then muttered, "Where am I? Who am I? What am I doing? Who… who are you?"

Memory loss. Although weak and confused, he was putting up a good fight.

The Froddy Guards re-joined them after having performed some heroics of their own. Circled by the water voles, they passed a note from Tommy to Tad, which had floated to the top. The wording was clear: it must only be given to Tad. They felt this was as good a time as any.

Dearest little brother, Tad,

I've done this for you all, but first and foremost, for you. There will not be enough air parcels for everyone. The surface will be too deep for others to get to the top and breathe again. Take my share and ask the elders to do the same. It should be enough to see many, especially the little ones, escape in one piece to their new home, sweet home.

Our cousins will not have this problem – they have supernatural lungs and bodies, just like you, and are protected no matter what happens. You know that already. However, they will need urgent warmth as soon as the water goes down. You, the Chosen One, must make sure they get it. Remember you can go anywhere and do anything. Be a light to the world, a beacon. The darkness of this world can never put it out. Save them…

Should I not survive this ordeal, do not worry. I am well cared for.

Goodbye and God bless. Keep your faith and keep smiling.

Yours with much love and tenderness,

Brother Tommy xx

Tad sobbed uncontrollably – they all did, touched by a love beyond words and overwhelmed with emotion. No one had been as brave and selfless as Tommy. He had been willing to make the ultimate sacrifice for others – his life.

Three

Time to Leave

The rain stopped. The waters would soon drop; enough for the Cloverdaisy Pond survivors to travel down the exit tunnel. They would all head there, and ultimately, the strong outward current would surge them to the safety and sanctuary of Frogstock Hall Pond – the final leg of their migration.

Splashing could be heard on the surface, and movement meant life. Powerful and strong, the bullfrogs and water voles could swim anywhere…and so they did. Tad decided to latch on, tucking in behind, while Tommy, still alive but critically ill, was left to recover on the bank, aided by none other than Neville and Fiona!

The water voles watched Tad closely, baffled. They couldn't fathom him out. He had no trouble keeping up with them and could stay under water much longer. What an enigma – was it purely miraculous? He seemed to be just a humble frog, but he was definitely different.

They stopped for a quick pow-wow to discuss the next move. The bullfrogs and water voles became scouts, acting like the raven and dove that were the first to leave Noah's Ark after the great flood in the Bible. Would they return?

"Let's continue!" boomed the bullfrogs. "Water voles away! Lead with your teeth."

"Right, lads," shouted Tad, "let's finish the job."

After a few yards, they came across the first survivors: a posse of tadpoles, dozens of baby frogs, tiny shoals of fish and loads of jelly-balls – frogspawn all in one piece.

Tad smiled then signalled, "Thirty minutes to the escape." The baby frogs nodded – they understood his language as one of their own.

The bullfrogs and the water voles zoomed on at speeds up to 25 mph, while Tad coasted behind. The voles' teeth could slice through anything so nothing would block their way, not even rock or metal. They were delighted to see that other species had survived, although they were exhausted by the ordeal.

Tad hollered, "When you hear the bugle call, please swim over to the far end of the pond and bring all the life craft over…at least, what's left of them." Then he returned to HQ with the Mighty Six. The Froddy Guards saw to Tommy first – sadly, Fiona and Neville had mysteriously disappeared, assumed drowned after struggling to help their own kind and selflessly seeing to Tommy. Strapping

Tommy to a stretcher, they got him ready to enter the tunnel.

Back at base, Tad prepared to make the call. He and the other leaders gathered for the last time before the finale.

"For vantage and safety reasons, I've now chosen the stream outlet to the pond to conduct the evacuation. If we go in the middle, we could get ambushed by flying predators. We dare not take the risk. They will be even more hungry now. Wait your turn by the edge, but do not panic as that might ruin everything.

"When everyone's assembled, I will create a massive whirlpool from the middle of the pond. It will make a huge current, which will act as a buffer between us and any unwanted attention – if predators try to pounce, they will be sucked in and drown. Wait one last time for the call. It will sound like the American military – US Froddy Guards, you will know exactly what I'm talking about."

"Yes, sir, we do, sir. Thank you, sir," came the disciplined reply.

"All aboard and away, me hearties! Jump on the life craft. There's plenty of oxygen in the tunnel – air holes lead up to the ground above. However, fill your lungs before going in. The water will be at its deepest there."

The burning question arose as to who would go down first of their kind. Tad hoped a volunteer would step forward from the Mighty Six, and sure enough, one did: the very brave Raj Water Vole. He had been

126

a real Maharajah, a great ruler, back in India, and now he was to be a great leader in England; a hero. He had rescued many creatures already, risking life and limb every time he dived, but he was cold having been out of the warmth for too long. Far longer than his brothers. He needed the heat of the aquarium quickly, or he would die.

Tad decided to go last like a true captain. Tommy would want that. He charged the Froddy Guards with Tommy's care, realising the sooner they got him through, the better. He then beckoned to all his companions and the other clans. The bugle call, played on a reed, would be their cue to leave as quickly as possible, and it would soon sound. The timing to engage the surge of floodwater had to be right.

Tad ordered everyone to gather and gorge on what food was left. They would need as much sustenance as possible. He then dived into the pond. Dipping his entire body deep into the water, he made a strange howling call, speaking in mysterious tongues. As he did so his magic tail spun like a helicopter blade, thousands and thousands of times; so fast that it looked like it wasn't moving!

Whirlpools, masses of them, and deep currents swirled and spun above and below the pond, miraculously stopping short of where everyone waited. Tad's whole body kept changing colour like a chameleon, then settled on the colours of the rainbow, again. The other leaders watched, fascinated.

The only danger left now was in the tunnel.

Heartbroken at what might happen to their brother-in-arms, Raj, the other two water voles stood by Am, Phib and Ian, readying themselves for the final part of the exodus. It would take one more huge, herculean effort to conquer the long tunnel.

Tad returned through the whirlpools, then jumped on top of the large pipe. He pursed his lips around a makeshift reed trumpet and sounded the reveille – "Dum-dum diddle um, dum-dum diddle um."

Then he hollered, "Dive, dive, dive!" like a submarine captain. "Stick to the middle and go with the flow. Make no attempt to resist it. Raj will lead our lot from the front, behind all the Fionas and Nevilles. Follow him closely, making sure you keep up."

With the command, all the pond life jumped into their life craft and shot into the water like triathletes. Half the original number had made it this far and were keen to go. To speed things up, Tad created even more super undercurrents at the front for Raj to ride on. He was first down, followed by the stretchered Tommy, heavily bandaged but just about conscious. Time was against him, though, and he was losing blood again.

Tad hoped Raj would get to the other side quickly and recharge his body heat, but the tunnel was over a mile long. He had hoped that nothing serious was blocking it, or, worse still, that it had collapsed during the storm. That would be fatal for them all, not just Tommy. The signs, however, were encouraging – there was a strong flow surging through the entrance, which suggested they would have a clear run. So far, so good.

Others followed, strapped to vine and reed. Then came the last battalion of survivors armed with life rafts and makeshift canoes. Their timing was perfect. Raj would be well away now, so Tad created one more huge whirlpool to push those behind more quickly. He and the other five leaders watched by the entrance, saluting everyone off.

Finally, it was Tad's turn. By this time, the other five had already headed back to the farm aquarium for urgent warmth. They had done their bit, and done it well.

The dark tunnel ride was like a long water chute – heart stopping, exhilarating and fast! However, Tad realised this was no fairground ride but a journey to freedom and new life. After about thirty minutes of riding the fast flowing cold water, he saw daylight filtering through at the other end as if a candle had just been lit. The journey was almost over.

Tad emerged, the last through. There were obvious casualties from the trip. Dead bodies had floated through the tunnel before and after them, mostly the very old, sick and young. Those who'd arrived safely had flopped and collapsed, half dead, on the bank. There was little sign of life – most of the survivors seemed content just to catch their breath and stare, totally disorientated. No one seemed bothered about an unusual feather-wrapped thermal parcel, slumped at the top of the bank beneath a willow tree.

Tad hopped over and stared at the parcel. An expressionless but recognisable head suddenly poked out from one end. Tad moved closer and gave it a nudge. It was Raj, groggy but alive. What a pleasant surprise, but how bizarre. Who had wrapped him up?

Raj opened his eyes briefly to see Tad smiling. Comforted by Tad's presence, he drifted back to sleep, but not before giving Tad another note from Tommy. Tad smiled again but did not read it. Humbled and exhausted by his lead role, he lay back to rest.

Suddenly he felt isolated, confused and frightened, but didn't know why. The atmosphere was surreal: opaque, hauntingly quiet and eerie. Something hidden was watching them.

Where was Tommy? Had kind pond locals or the afterlife taken him? Tad's sixth sense told him Tommy was still alive, but where? And why did he feel so low? Would they ever meet again? Questions and more questions! Maybe the euphoria of the migration had simply deserted him.

The clouds burst open and it rained again, hard. Tad looked up, then back to ground level. Moments later, he saw something which lifted his spirits and gladdened his heart: on the opposite bank, surviving clans had started to build fresh homes in their new surroundings. The success of the migration was already bearing fruit aplenty.

As he watched, some creatures waved back and smiled, others gave him a 'thumbs up'. Finally, he gave in to the wave of exhaustion and crashed out. The mix of emotions lulled him into dreamy thoughts. Time, like the tide, had waited for none of them, not even Tad.

However, this was not the end; it was merely the beginning. From tadpole to frogling, Tad had evolved into a fully-grown super-frog. He had arrived. Tad had become the supreme leader and from this day, all things were now possible; the day when Cloverdaisy village pond was now no more.

The Mystery of Cloverdaisy Cottage

Part Two – The Enchanted Pond

One

Return to the Loft

Kate finished, tired but thrilled. She looked to see Clara, her mum Ruth and Nanna Grace in tears. She too was sobbing, having found some pages difficult to read. Through each one, she had imagined Pops hunched over his old typewriter, copying text from his rough longhand notes. They were all so very proud. He was truly a special man.

Kate eventually spoke. "That's the most beautiful story I have ever read or heard. Little Ollie will love it when he's older – what a smashing way to get to know Pops."

"So fascinating," said Clara, smiling sweetly. "This deserves to get published quickly."

Nanna Grace sat back and sobbed even more, as did Ruth.

"That would be amazing," said Kate. "What do you think, Nanna?"

"About what, dear?" asked Nanna Grace, blowing her

nose with a huge trumpety sound.

"Nanna, do please listen! About getting Grandpa Pops's story published?"

Nanna Grace lifted her head up, dried her tears and leaned forward. Gathering her thoughts and composure, she replied somewhat haughtily, "Well, I don't like the thought of my dear Gilbert's enchanting manuscript being sent to a stranger. It's so precious now, girls, and so beautifully read by you, granddaughter. Well done, Kate, you should be on the TV."

"A publisher will look after it, Nanna, I promise..."

"We'll see," said Nanna Grace in a voice that invited no argument. "For now, I want to know it's safely stored away in Pops's chest in the loft. Put it back there, please, girls."

"And be careful!" said Ruth, still giddy from the reading.

"Of course we will," said Clara, taking the manuscript from the table. Kate joined her as they walked slowly across the kitchen floor before flying back up the staircase.

"Wow!" said Kate. "Imagine Pops being published."

"Don't you have to be famous to get that done?" asked Clara.

"No, not really," replied Kate, adamantly. "How do you think all those other authors we read got famous? They had to start somewhere."

"True," said Clara, pushing the lid up again to get back into the loft.

They crept and crawled gently over the squeaky floorboards and put the manuscript back in the chest. As they did so, a very strange thing happened. A rainbow-shaped beam of light hit the floor, and right in the middle appeared the

image of a Golden Frog. As if that wasn't spooky enough, the girls clearly heard him speak.

"Hello again, Clara."

Kate stared in awe at Clara.

The frog laughed, a funny croaking sound that made the girls smile despite their astonishment.

"What on earth is that?" asked Kate. "How does it know your name, Clara?"

"Because, um, we've met before," mumbled Clara, looking away from her friend. "He, um, showed me where to look for the manuscript. Then he vanished."

"He showed you…Then he…My goodness, Clara, I think you've gone mad!"

"That's why I didn't tell you!" exclaimed Clara angrily. "I knew you would think that."

"Now, now, girls," croaked the Golden Frog. "Don't let's argue."

"Sorry, Tad," said Clara without thinking.

"What did you say?" shrieked Kate.

"Just a guess," replied Clara sheepishly. "After all, he was a golden frog too."

"Good guess," said the Golden Frog, bowing to Clara. Turning around, he then hopped across the room.

"Look!" Kate shouted. "Over there in the dim corner. He's beckoning us to follow him. It's so scary. Let's get back… I don't like this…"

"It is scary," said Clara, "but we can't go yet. This is incredible, miraculous – a message from beyond, perhaps."

"Beyond? Beyond what?"

"Now look – he's bringing over a red rose."

The girls tiptoed over, cautiously. As they leaned forward to receive the rose, the floorboards gave way, leaving them

floating…down…down…down into the bowels of the cellar hidden beneath the cottage.

"Whoa, please stop. Please!" they shouted, but they didn't

stop. Instead, they plummeted into a long, dark tunnel.

"I feel like Alice," hollered Clara, "when she tumbles down that rabbit hole to Wonderland."

Suddenly…crash, bang, wallop! They arrived right in front of a huge coloured aquarium split into three. It was full of exotic looking fish, bullfrogs, water voles and all manner of amphibian life.

Kate spoke hesitantly. "Wow, this must be Jack's aquarium. The one he never lets anyone see. How on earth did we get here? Are we dreaming?"

She felt a tug at her pocket and something thorny and sweet smelling tangled in her hair.

"Ouch!" she said, grabbing hold of the red rose and pricking her finger on the thorns. "No, we're not dreaming. That really hurt."

Looking up, she saw the Golden Frog vanish around the back of the aquarium. She and Clara crawled over to find a small medical cubicle tucked away with a curtain around it. A large green frog was lying in a hospital bed in the middle, a card around his neck saying, Tommy, Frog Hero.

"It's Tommy Frog," said Kate. "So he did survive. And look, by the side of the curtain – it's the Golden Frog himself, Tad. Mind boggling!"

"What's he showing us now?" asked Clara as Tad beckoned them closer. "Well I never! I wonder where that leads."

The girls found themselves peering at the entrance to another tunnel, warmly lit with green lamps and inviting them in.

"Frogstock Pond," Tad replied proudly. "Come and visit…"

Tad was interrupted by the sound of a door opening, then slamming shut. An angry voice that sounded much like

Jack's, exclaimed, "What on earth are you doing here?" then the whole room started to spin. The aquarium, voles, frogs and hospital became a blur as it whizzed faster and faster.

Just as the girls thought they were going to be sick, everything swirled and went black.

"What on earth happened?" asked Kate, sitting up in the loft of Nanna Grace's cottage and rubbing the back of her head ruefully.

"Well I don't know about you, but I went with Tad to visit Tommy Frog in hospital."

"You were with me? So it really did happen?"

"Yes!" said Clara emphatically. "And I can prove it. Look!"

Following the direction of Clara's pointing finger, Kate looked at the floorboards in the corner of the loft, which had collapsed and hurtled them into the cellar.

"Oh my goodness! How are we going to explain that to Nanna?" Then she looked down at her hand, which was still clutching the red rose.

"Wow!" she whispered in amazement, grinning as the memory struck her. "That Golden Frog...sorry, Tad, put something in my pocket too. Look!"

Kate rummaged in her pocket, unfurling a crumpled piece of paper. She held it up, hoping to see better. The writing on it was scrawly and written in Old English. Clara sat up and listened as Kate read out what was on it.

Dearest granddaughter, Kate, and your best friend, Clara,

Sorry I cannot be with you anymore, but I am in spirit. You have got this far for a reason and done really well. You are near to finishing the story of Cloverdaisy Pond, and completing the journey of my manuscript. The Golden Frog will help you finish the task.

Tommy is struggling to recover...he does not have long.

He possesses some of Tad's powers, but does not have the ultimate gift of eternal life.

Many long years ago, mystical gifts were bestowed upon the Cloverdaisy Pond life here by the Abbey monks. Saints of old kept these gifts alive for centuries, and we have the farmer's son, Jack, to thank for keeping the tradition alive – literally. He shelters and preserves all rare pond life, ensuring the creatures can breed safely and live as one. My manuscript will have told you much more about the story – I hope you enjoyed reading it as much as I enjoyed writing it and hearing it again. But it's not quite over.

Nanna Grace, I suspect, always knew far more than I let on. Please tell her of my love for her and you all. The gypsy love prayer says it all. You will find it in the Bible in my daughter's name: 'Wherever you go, I will go. Wherever you live, I will live, and our love will be the gift of all our lives.'

God be with you till we meet again.

Your dearest, Grandpa Pops xxx

PS. Make sure you give Nanna Grace the rose.

Both girls were crying by the time Kate had finished reading, and neither of them could speak for a few moments.

"My goodness," said Clara through her tears. "A note from beyond the grave, how wonderful." Wiping her eyes, she suddenly stared at Kate as another thought struck her. "It must have been Pops's voice I heard…"

"What voice?" asked Kate sharply. "When did you hear a voice?"

"Before we first came into the loft," Clara replied sheepishly. Then again when I found the manuscript. A ghostly voice told me to follow the frog."

"Why didn't you…OK, I think I can guess. You didn't tell me because you didn't want me to think you were insane. Quite frankly, after today I'll never think anything is insane again! So, what did the voice say when you found the manuscript?"

"It said, 'At last you've found me'."

"It must have been Grandpa Pops, then! Why didn't he speak to me?"

"Probably because…"

"I'd have thought I was crazy!"

Both girls burst into helpless laughter, only managing to control themselves when Ruth yelled up at them through the hatch.

"What are you up to in there? You've been gone ages."

"Coming, Mum," called Kate as she and Clara scrambled across what remained of the floorboards. Leaving the enchanted loft behind, they clambered back down the ladder to the everyday world below.

Two

An Angry Farmer

"Where did you find this?" asked Nanna Grace. "And that lovely red rose?" She had read Grandpa Pops's letter many times in the last half hour and had only just composed herself enough to speak.

"In the loft, Nanna," replied Kate. After Clara saying how worried she'd been that everyone would think her nuts if she told them about spooky voices and vanishing frogs, Kate was too embarrassed to tell Nanna Grace the whole truth.

"But it's from Gilbert. How...how can he write a letter and give me a rose when he's...passed..." Then Nanna Grace visibly made an effort to pull herself together. "The cunning old fox! I always knew he would get a message to me, even after he'd gone, but not like that. It's beautiful, girls, and so touching."

Sighing, Nanna Grace peered out of the window as Ruth entered the room. She'd been rootling around upstairs the whole time Nanna had been reading the letter from Pops and did not look happy.

"OK, girls," she said sternly, "I think you have a confession to make, don't you?"

The girls blushed bright red. They knew exactly what was coming.

"Mum," continued Ruth, attracting Nanna Grace's attention, "there's a great big hole in your bedroom ceiling!"

"There's a what?"

Kate and Clara, both clearly embarrassed, tried to explain at the same time.

"We were following the Golden Frog..."

"We couldn't help it, they just gave way..."

"We fell into the cellar, then the tunnel..."

"Then the aquarium where Tommy Frog is in hospital..."

"He's dying, Nanna. Then Tad gave me the note..."

"And the rose. Tad gave her the rose from Pops, Nanna Grace..."

"Stop!" roared Ruth, holding up her hand. "What is all this nonsense?"

"It's not nonsense," said Nanna Grace quietly. "Gilbert... your father often said he chatted to Tad in the loft. You see, towards the end he wasn't well enough to visit Frogstock Pond any more, but he always made the effort to go into the loft to keep up with the latest news from Frogstock."

Ruth looked at her mother, her face a mass of emotions. First confusion, then disbelief, then anger, wonder and confusion again.

"But it's just a fairy story," she said eventually. "A fantasy… isn't it?"

Three earnest faces gazed back at her. In the end all she could say was, "Oh my."

"Nanna," said Kate, "I'm so sorry about the loft falling into your bedroom…"

"Shh!" snapped Nanna Grace. "I'm thinking." Ruth, Kate and Clara waited in silence as Nanna Grace screwed up her face in concentration. Finally, her brow unfurrowed a little and she looked at the girls.

"Kate, Clara, did you find anything else of interest in the loft? Not that the manuscript and this lovely letter and rose aren't interesting. Of course they are. Very. Oh, Gilbert, my dear Gilbert…"

Again, she lapsed into deafening silence for a few moments before saying, "Grandpa Pops always said he'd stored something up there. Something valuable. 'Save it for a rainy day,' he would say, but I can't for the life of me remember whether he ever told me what it was."

"Well," said Kate hesitantly, "there are some old toys…"

"Toys!" crowed baby Ollie, choosing that moment to wake up from his nap in his buggy. "Ollie 'ont toys!"

"Well, it looks like you'd better go and fetch them, girls," said Ruth, still looking dazed as she lifted the little boy into her arms. "Ollie won't be happy until he's had a look."

The girls made their weary way back to the haunted loft.

"We might as well live here," grumbled Kate, shoving the hatch across and scrambling through. "We spend that much time in it. This is our fourth visit today."

"I'll stay down here," suggested Clara, "and you can pass the toys to me."

"Umm," said Kate dubiously.

"Not afraid of the ghosts, are you?" asked Clara, laughing. This hurt Kate's pride.

"No I am not!" she retorted. "You stay there then, scaredy cat, and I'll pass the toys down to you."

"That's what I said," muttered Clara, but Kate had already crawled into the depths of the loft where the toys were concealed. One by one she passed them down to Clara – a china doll and a ragged old teddy bear, a wooden train, a spinning top, some toy soldiers and another teddy bear, this one in much better condition than the first. Then she climbed down herself and closed the hatch.

Looking down at the haul, she said, "I can't see this lot being worth much. At least they've been covered in a dust sheet so they're not as filthy as everything else up there."

"Come on," said Clara. "Let's take them down."

They could hear Ollie was getting impatient, but as they slithered down the stairs, their arms full of toys, his cries were drowned out by a hammering on the door.

"Get that, would you, Kate?" called Ruth.

"Can't, Mum. Hands full."

Grumbling, Ruth stomped out of the kitchen to answer the door, Ollie protesting in her arms. As soon as he saw his sister and her best friend laden with toys, his cries turned to squeals of delight. He struggled from Ruth's grasp and scrambled after the girls with arms outstretched.

Dumping the toys on the kitchen table, the girls passed them to Ollie one by one. His eyes lit up when he saw the train. Nanna Grace scanned the rest of the toys with misty but inquisitive eyes.

"Goodness," she said. "Some of these must have belonged to Grandpa Pops, and this china doll to his mother, Molly."

"But will they be worth any...?"

Kate was cut short by a baffled looking Ruth, re-entering the kitchen with Jack the farmer in tow.

"Er, Jack says that..." began Ruth, but Jack interrupted furiously.

"What the devil were you doing earlier?" he bellowed, glaring at the girls.

"Don't know what you mean."

"Yes you do! My aquarium is private. Off limits. Secret." Jack stopped his rant as a thought struck him. "Yes, secret, so how on earth did you find it?"

"Umm..."

"Errr..."

"Tad showed us," mumbled Kate eventually.

"Oh no, not this nonsense again," said Ruth, but the effect of Kate's words on Jack took them all by surprise. He staggered back as if someone had punched him, all the anger draining from him in an instant.

"Tad," he gasped. "You've met Tad? Well, I should have known really. After all, you are Gilbert's granddaughter."

"Actually, it was Clara who saw him first," admitted Kate.

"That doesn't surprise me either," said Jack, grinning at the girls' quizzical expressions. "You and Kate are more alike than you think. You're both psychic."

Ruth was beginning to feel faint. She steadied herself by

leaning against the kitchen table. "Does anyone want a cup of tea?" she asked, absently passing a teddy bear into Ollie's eager hands. "Because I need a strong one."

"Ruth, don't give that to Ollie!" commanded Jack. Ruth took the bear back from Ollie, much to his vocal dismay, hastily replacing it with a toy soldier. Taking the teddy bear gently, Jack examined it, then looked up at Ruth with excited eyes.

"I'm no expert, so you'll need to get this checked out, but I'm pretty sure this is a very old Steiff bear. A rare one. I'm a bit of a fan of antiques programmes and toys crop up occasionally. There was talk of a missing Steiff bear only last year, and it is believed to be worth a fortune."

"Do you think that might be the missing one?" asked Kate.

"I'm sure of it," replied Nanna Grace before Jack could speak. "Remember what Grandpa Pops told me?"

"That he'd stored something valuable in the loft for a rainy day?"

"That's right, and I think you might just have found it. After all, the loft does seem to have a knack for guiding you to the right things at the right time."

"With the help of Tad," said Clara.

"And Grandpa's voice," added Kate, grinning at her friend.

"So, Jack," said Nanna Grace, the pragmatic one for once, "if this is that rare stiff bear..."

"Steiff," corrected Jack.

"That's what I said," snapped Nanna Grace. "If this is that rare stiff bear, how much will it be worth? Hundreds of pounds?"

"No," said Jack, "more!"

"What? Wow!" chorused everyone in the kitchen, apart from Ollie who was busy trying to make the toy soldiers stand up.

"Actually," continued Jack, milking the moment, "more like thousands of pounds."

Three

Intruders on the Farm

As the halcyon days of the girls' summer holiday passed in a blaze of sunshine and fun, the teddy bear was sent securely to experts in Germany for verification and assessment. After a couple of weeks, the report finally came through by courier, such was its importance.

It turned out that it was indeed a rare vintage Steiff bear, one of the oldest in the world, and worth an absolute fortune. The experts had even located the original trademark stitched into one of its ears, unusual for this type of bear but one hundred per cent genuine. It was well over 100 years old. The price it fetched was more than enough to do up the whole of Cloverdaisy Cottage, not just the hole in Nanna Grace's bedroom ceiling! She often wondered where Grandpa Pops had got it from in the first place, but reckoned she'd now never know – unless she asked Tad, of course.

While the restoration work was taking place in her cottage, Nanna Grace moved into one of the spare rooms in Cloverdaisy farmhouse. In return for her cosy room and hearty meals, she continued to help Jack on the farm, usually with the milking but sometimes with the upkeep of the secret aquarium that had been crucial to the escape from Cloverdaisy Pond.

Tad also spent much of his time at the aquarium, keeping an eye on Tommy and chatting happily with Jack, the Froddy Guards and the Indian water voles. The original heroes from The Escape were getting on a bit in years now, but they never tired of telling the story to their own children and grandchildren – or to Nanna Grace's granddaughter and best friend, for that matter. Unsurprisingly, Kate and Clara were daily visitors to the farm.

"Bye, Mum," called Kate to Ruth one morning, shortly before the start of the new school term, as she opened the door to an excited Clara. As usual, the girls couldn't wait to get to the farm and continue their search for Frogstock Pond.

"Wait a moment," said Ruth, bustling through from the kitchen with Ollie clinging on to one hand and the girls' packed lunches in the other. "You can't expect Jack to feed you all the time, and no doubt I won't see either of you again until evening."

Grinning, Kate took the lunches with a kiss for Ruth and Ollie and a "Thank you, Mum," before dashing out into the sunshine. "Bye everyone!" shouted Clara. Running all the way to Cloverdaisy Farm, the girls arrived breathless and debated whether to go to the farmhouse first or make the most of the good weather.

"I say we search straight away," said Clara. "It's got to be around here somewhere."

The pond itself had never got built on due to continuous

flooding and was now, very fittingly, a wildlife reserve, making their search harder. Knowing what they did about its original location, the girls had narrowed their exploration to a small area close to Cloverdaisy Farm. However, they had already hunted high and low, but had still not found any sign of a pond, enchanted or otherwise, anywhere near the farm.

"There's that couple again," said Kate with a slight frown, shading her eyes and peering at the man and woman who always seemed to be searching the area too. "They're here every day. Wonder if Nanna Grace has seen them again?"

"It's a bit suspicious," said Clara. "Oh look! They've spotted you and scuttled off again."

"They do that every time. I think we ought to tell Jack. There's something very fishy about them, especially the woman."

"I think the man looks like a slippery character too," said Clara. "Let's go and tell Jack right now. They might be kidnappers."

"Or murderers," agreed Kate with a shudder. "Come on, let's go."

Abandoning their search, Kate and Clara sped off to the farmhouse. Nanna Grace was in the kitchen enjoying a cup of tea, but there was no sign of Jack.

"Nanna Grace, where's Jack? We've got something to tell him."

"He's in the aquarium, girls, as usual," she said with a wry smile. "Don't worry, I didn't think you'd come to see me."

Looking sheepish, the girls shuffled their feet until Nanna Grace stood up, rinsed out her cup and said, "Come on.

157

You know the way to the secret passage."

Thundering down the cellar steps, with Nanna Grace following on at a more sedate pace, Kate and Clara ran towards what looked like a solid brick wall.

"I love this bit," said Clara, appearing to go right through it.

"It's almost like the wardrobe that leads to Narnia," added Kate, following Clara through the wall, which wasn't a wall at all but the disguised mouth of a short tunnel – the only way into the enchanted aquarium.

"Morning, girls," said Jack cheerfully as he busied himself helping Tad and the water voles to clean out the aquarium.

"Morning, girls," echoed Tad in his trademark croak. "Morning, Nanna Grace."

"Morning, Jack, Tad, voles and bullfrogs, everyone," echoed the girls. Nanna Grace, who had followed them into room, simply nodded elegantly and busied herself preparing assorted goodies for the aquarium creatures' lunches.

"Tad has just been telling me that you still haven't been to visit Frogstock Pond," said Jack. "I thought you'd have been straight over there."

"Mum and Dad can't wait to meet you," added Tad.

"We're trying, Tad, really we are, but we can't find it anywhere." Nanna said. "If we can't find a way then make one!"

Tad's bulbous eyes rolled heavenwards, and Jack grinned knowingly at him.

"Think you're going to have to tell them, Tad, old friend."

"I've already shown you," said Tad, turning his exasperation on the girls. "Nanna Grace tells me you're super intelligent, so I thought you'd be able to work it out."

"You've shown us? Oh!" The realisation dawned on Kate and Clara at the same time as Tad stared pointedly at the corner of the room behind Tommy's hospital bed beside his heart machine.

"It's hidden by enchantments, isn't it?" said Kate. "Just like this aquarium. You can't find it unless you know where the entrance is."

"Correct!" said Tad, doing his best to make his froggy croak sound like the authoritative voice of a headmaster. As he spoke, the tunnel became illuminated once again with the same friendly green lights the girls remembered from their first visit, when they'd fallen so inelegantly through the rotten floorboards in the haunted loft. Just as they were about to disappear down the tunnel, though, Nanna Grace pulled them up short.

"Wait a minute, girls. Didn't you have something important to tell Jack?"

"Oh yes," said Kate, doing an about turn and trotting back into the room with Clara close on her heels. "We keep seeing two people, a man and a woman, hanging around the farm."

"They seem to be looking for something..."

"Yes, and they're searching in exactly the place where we worked out that Frogstock Pond should be."

"Sounds fishy to me," said Jack, scratching his chin and glancing at Tad. His amphibian friend was looking thoughtful. "What is it, Tad?"

"What do these people look like?" Tad asked.

"Well," said Kate, "the woman is not the prettiest in the

159

world. She's got the biggest mouth I've ever seen – great big chopses, as Nanna would say."

"And bad skin," added Clara. "Almost scaly."

"The man has a long nose, oily face and great bulbous eyes…"

"Nothing wrong with that," said Tad with a sniff and a snot.

"…set quite wide apart…"

"Nothing wrong with that, either…" began Tad, but Jack interrupted.

"I don't believe it! I've told them to stay away, but they keep coming back."

"Oh, do you know who they are?" asked Clara.

"I do indeed," growled Jack.

"Kidnappers?"

"No."

"Murderers?"

"No, girls! Don't you think I would tell the police if kidnappers and murderers were hanging around my farm?"

The girls giggled.

"No, they are none other than Fiona and Neville."

"Fiona and Neville? No wonder she looks fishy!"

"And no wonder he looks slimy!"

"Excuse me, what's wrong with being slimy?" asked Tad, rolling his hand down the front of his puffed up chest and looking a bit put out.

"Right, I'm going to sort that pesky pair out once and for all. They're looking for Frogstock Pond, but they will not find it."

"Show him the letter, Tad," came a feeble croak from the

hospital bed in front of the tunnel entrance. Tommy had got weaker.

Without a word, Tad got up from his seat and hopped

over to where he lay. Opening the cabinet by the side of his bed, he took out a letter then handed it to Jack.

"Tommy gave this to me when he thought he wasn't going to pull through. We're so lucky that he's survived all these years after the awful injuries he sustained during the escape."

Jack took the letter and unfolded it. "It's all in Frogish!" he exclaimed.

"So? You speak Frogish."

"Yes, Tad, but I can't read it."

Taking the letter back, Tad read it out. The bullfrogs and Froddy Guards crowded round too, anxious to piece together the missing parts of that horrible night they saved the lives of so many Cloverdaisy Pond dwellers.

Dear Tad,

This has been a night of excitement, adventure and enchantment. So much has happened and so many have shown the utmost courage. I commend every single one of you, but it doesn't end there.

Fiona and Neville – how we misjudged them. In my hour of need, seriously injured and not expecting to make it even this far, they have tended to me gently and kindly. Not only that, they have shown themselves to be compassionate beyond compare as they have put their lives at risk to care for all the injured. When Raj and I appeared from the mouth of the tunnel, Fiona and Neville were already in Frogstock Pond. They went on ahead when they realised I was adequately cared for by you and the other leaders, clearing the way as much as they could. Despite being exhausted from their own efforts, they saw that Raj was in a bad way, seriously cold and close to losing consciousness, and they wrapped him up as warmly as they could in the feathers Neville found in an abandoned swans' nest nearby. Had it not been for their quick thinking, he would certainly have died.

Tad, I feel that you still don't know your true power. You prayed for as many of us as possible to survive this night, and your prayer was answered. In the chaos of everyone pouring through the tunnel from Cloverdaisy, no one but I noticed Fiona and Neville struggling for their own lives having helped so many others to survive. I was too sick to help. As a fish and a newt, they couldn't survive. As humans, they could.

Your special magic saved them as they saved me, your loving brother. They walked away from Frogstock to begin a new life in the human world. But one day, when the time is right, they will return. They must return. Our story deserves to be told.

My dearest brother, if I don't live to see this time, I know you will do the right thing.

Your ever loving, Tommy xx

There was a reverent hush over the aquarium as the words of Tommy's letter filtered through. The silence was so complete, it took a few moments for its significance to sink in. The beep-beep-beep of Tommy's heart monitor stopped.

"No!" cried Tad, bounding across the room in one huge hop to land at his brother's bedside. "No, no, no!"

Creatures and humans alike bowed their heads in respect as a distraught Tad kissed his brother's forehead, gently closed Tommy's eyes then covered his head with the bed sheet. He looked down at the shrouded body of the bravest frog he'd ever known, then composed himself and raised his tearful eyes to the company in the aquarium.

"Tommy's wish is about to be granted," he said. "The time has come. Let's go and find Fiona and Neville."

Four

Return to Frogstock

It was quite a crowd that emerged from the farmhouse five minutes later. Jack, Nanna Grace and the two girls were joined by Tad, who rarely went into the everyday world since Cloverdaisy's flooding, the Froddy Guards and Indian water voles.

"Where did you say you saw them?" asked Jack, looking towards the horizon.

"Over there," replied Kate, pointing. "That's where we reckoned Frogstock Pond should be."

"Goodness me, you're spot on," said Tad. "With powers of deduction that good, you two could end up being great detectives like Sherlock Holmes. That's where Frogstock Pond is, but you have to use the correct entrance, or else it isn't."

"Isn't what."

"Isn't there. It's only there if you use the enchanted entrance. See?"

"No!" said Kate.

"Look," cried Clara, flapping her hands madly at a couple of people creeping furtively over the hill behind where Frogstock Pond should be. "Fiona and Neville."

"Don't let them see us," warned Jack, creeping behind a tractor and indicating that the others should do the same. "If they see me, they'll bolt off."

"Then I'll go," said Tad, hopping off before anyone could argue.

"I'm not missing this," said Kate.

"Me neither," added Clara as the girls set off in pursuit of Tad. However, the moment Neville and Fiona saw them, they turned to scarper.

"Fiona! Neville! Wait, wait!" called Tad at the top of his voice.

"Wait, Fiona and Neville!" hollered the girls. "Tad needs to speak to you."

At the name Tad, Fiona and Neville froze as if they'd just been turned into stone. Then slowly, oh so slowly, they faced the trio approaching them.

"T-Tad?" stammered Fiona. "Is that really you?"

"Am, Phib and Ian?" added Neville, looking beyond Tad and the girls. "And is that Raj, Saj and Taj? Can it be?"

The rest of the group from the aquarium had caught up with Tad and the girls, and now stood facing the startled Neville and Fiona. Eventually, Raj broke the tense silence.

"Fiona and Neville," he said, "I owe my life to you. What can I say? Thank you."

"It was nothing…"

"Nothing? But you nearly died, more than once."

"H-how did you know we hadn't?"

"Tommy told us everything in a letter he wrote that night. Here," said Tad, holding the precious letter from his brother, "read it."

Fiona unfolded the letter and scanned its contents. "It's all in Frogish," she said, disappointed.

Taking the letter back from her outstretched hand, Tad summarised its contents for them. "So you see," he said, "we know of your bravery and compassion that night. We know you almost lost your lives, and we know you have to tell the story of Cloverdaisy Pond. The time has come, my dear friends, for you to return to Frogstock."

Fiona and Neville looked at each other.

"We've been searching for years," said Neville. "Our instincts continually tell us to return, but we can't find our way."

"Well now you have," said Tad. "Come."

Turning, he hopped off in the direction of the farmhouse, glad to get his rapidly drying body out of the strong rays of the sun. As everyone else followed, Neville wondered out loud whether he and Fiona would be returning as humans or fish and newt.

"Humans," said Fiona emphatically before anyone else could reply. "We have a story to tell, remember?"

"Yes, and we're perfectly placed to tell it to the world!" added Neville gleefully, grinning around at his companions. "I'm a journalist, you see, for a national newspaper."

"And I'm an editor for the country's biggest publishing house," added Fiona proudly. Kate, Clara and Nanna Grace were all struck by her words at the same time.

"Fiona the lady editor!" exclaimed Nanna Grace. "Of course! You met my husband ages ago – he's already written the story."

"You must be Grace," said Fiona, her face shining with delight. "How I longed to read his manuscript, but he would never let me. I thought it must have been destroyed or gone to the afterlife."

"No, it's safe and secure in the farmhouse while my cottage is being renovated. I'm sorry, my dear, but he didn't seem to trust you. Said there was something fishy about you."

Fiona's laughter sounded like someone gargling.

"They don't come much fishier than me," she said, linking arms with Nanna Grace as they entered the farmhouse and made for the cellar. "Do you think you can trust me now?"

"I know I can," replied Nanna Grace, patting Fiona's cold hand. "Come on, it's time for you to go home."

Tad led his group of friends through the cheerfully green-lit tunnel to Frogstock Pond. They stopped as one, open mouthed with awe and wonder – it was so incredibly beautiful. The air was ringing with the cheerful sounds of birdsong and fragrant with the scent of flowers growing around the banks of the peaceful and tranquil pond. The water sparkled in the sunlight, reflecting the blue of the sky as it rippled in the gentle breeze. The banks were guarded by graceful weeping willows and beyond them the leaves of mighty oaks rustled. All around, pond creatures went about their business or simply basked in the sunshine.

"I'd forgotten how truly special it is," whispered Fiona.

"And how peaceful," added Neville.

"Look, there's a snake enjoying lunch with a mouse, not lunching on a mouse."

"And there's a heron telling a joke to a frog. A funny one, by the looks of it," Jack added as the frog roared with laughter, then turned in their direction. Leaping from lily pad to lily pad, he crossed the pond in a trice, calling and croaking to his wife as he went.

"Victoria! Victoria! They're here!"

From the depths of the pond, another frog appeared – elderly, but still strong. Delighted, Victoria and Albert greeted their son and bullfrog cousins warmly, not forgetting to include Jack and the Indian water voles, then turned to the other humans before them.

"I know you," said Victoria to Nanna Grace. "You used to come walking with that lovely man by Cloverdaisy when we were young frogs. What was his name, Albert?"

"Gilbert," replied Nanna Grace. "I know you, too. You, Albert and Gilbert would have such long conversations." A mischievous grin crossed Nanna Grace's face. "And I could understand every word."

"You never let on!" exclaimed Victoria as she and Nanna Grace collapsed into helpless giggles, an elderly frog and an elderly woman enjoying a perfect moment of bliss and friendship.

"And who are you?" asked Albert, turning to the two people standing in the background as the greetings and felicitations went on.

"Don't you recognise them, Dad?" asked Tad. "It's Fiona and Neville."

"We mean you no harm," said Neville hastily.

"I know that, my friend. We have no enemies here, as you can see." Albert illustrated this point by waving and calling, "See you next week, Henry," to the heron as he flew off. "Besides," he added, turning back to Neville and Fiona, "my son Tommy owes his life to you two."

"How is Tommy, anyway, Tad?" asked Victoria. Tad's face fell, the euphoria of the greetings crashing down into instant grief, and she knew. "He's gone," she whispered, looking up to the sky as she said it. There was no rainbow this time.

"Yes." Tad held his mother as she cried, giving her the time she needed to come to terms with the sad news. Albert remained solemn, mournful of expression.

"So it is time," she said finally.

"It is," said Tad. "That's why Fiona and Neville are here."

"I don't understand…"

"We're going to tell your story to the whole world," said Fiona. "Just like Tommy wanted."

Fiona and Neville were true to their word. Within a year, Grandpa Pops's story *The Cloverdaisy Escape* was a best-selling book in every English and Frogish speaking country in the world. Even the most famous movie director of the time was in talks with Nanna Grace, Ruth and Jack with a view to making a film of it. Whether Tad should be a part of these negotiations was debatable. The frog himself then decided that the film director might not be fluent in Frogish and he couldn't be doing with the hassle of a translator. Neville made sure Nanna Grace, who was loving her new-found fame and fortune, appeared on all her favourite television and radio programmes. She regularly featured in his newspaper, talking about farming techniques, amphibian rights, cottage renovation and...baking!

Cloverdaisy Cottage became as safe and cosy as it had ever been since its makeover. Nanna was always delighted to welcome the press photographers and TV cameramen in to have a look, while Kate and Clara made sure they got in as many film and photo shoots as possible – Nanna Grace wasn't the only one who'd been bitten by the fame bug! As a fitting backdrop, the living room shelves now proudly housed the books collected by her late husband. Next to these were the remains of the red rose and, in a gold picture frame, the letter from Pops. Oliver was allowed to keep his treasure – the worthless toy soldier – and Pops got a new headstone for his grave, for which Grace asked the girls to compose an epitaph:

> Here lies Pops, as pleased as punch.
> He always knew, we had a hunch,
> That mystery loft, those magic frogs,
> Would reappear from ghostly gods.

Only the old loft, left to the grime and soot and antiques once its floorboards had been replaced, remained out of bounds to the photographers and film crews. As the sound of laughter and the clink of champagne glasses (lemonade for Kate and Clara!) drifted up from downstairs, a sudden gust of wind blew across the floor. Clouds of dust were whipped up, disturbing a medieval curtain hanging from the loft window, bearing the famous Coat of Arms of King Edward I.

In the corner of the curtain was the faint image of a nun.

A black silk scarf draped around her neck and shoulders was embroidered with the Latin words: *Te amo ab imo pectore – nunc scio quid sit amor.*

I love you all from the bottom of my heart – now I know what love really is.

The wind eased and the curtain settled back over the window. As the dust coated the loft once more, a faint glow shone from inside the ancient writing desk behind which Kate had originally stashed the valuable Steiff teddy bear. It lasted just a few seconds before the gloom returned, and besides, there was no one left in the loft now to notice it... Not this time, anyway.